College Basketball: Wagering to Win

by
Larry R. Seidel

authorHOUSE™

1663 LIBERTY DRIVE, SUITE 200
BLOOMINGTON, INDIANA 47403
(800) 839-8640
WWW.AUTHORHOUSE.COM

First published by AuthorHouse 08/12/05

ISBN: 1-4208-7295-8 (sc)

Library of Congress Control Number: 2005906787

Printed in the United States of America
Bloomington, Indiana

This book is printed on acid-free paper.

Contents

1. The Opportunity for Fun and Profit

Fans who wager on college basketball can become consistent winners and still gain the full entertainment value of both the games and wagering.

This book is for fans that enjoy wagering on college basketball. While wagering primarily for entertainment, they would prefer to win, rather than lose, and are willing to invest a modest amount of time to do the work that it takes to become a consistent winner.

Wagering provides wonderful entertainment value for college basketball fans. They can enjoy watching a game and placing money at risk, and without trying too hard, they can win more than half of their point spread bets. Very few people who go to the movies, the ballet, a rock concert, a museum or the most awesome parties ever walk out with more money than they had when they walked in!

College basketball has become a very popular source of entertainment. There are more teams than ever and those teams are drawing bigger crowds. The comprehensive media coverage of college basketball—television, radio, newspapers and Internet websites— is unprecedented.

The media gives you the opportunity to watch or listen to hundreds of games each week of the season. The Internet makes it possible for you to listen to most of the games of your favorite team, regardless of where you live. In the next few years, you probably will be able to watch most of the games of your favorite team.

At the same time, opportunities for fans to wager on college basketball games have increased to levels that could only be imagined a few years ago. The emergence of offshore sports books has provided fans with a means to wager on games that is far superior in every way to a local bookie. The hundreds of offshore sports books, many of which are licensed by foreign governments, provide a robust wagering market that operates like other markets where there are buyers and sellers. And, of course, sports books in Nevada continue to grow in terms of patrons and total bets handled.

There is a simple, but important, relationship between media coverage of college basketball and wagering on the sport. When fans watch or listen to a college basketball game many want to increase their enjoyment by wagering on it. Conversely, if a fan places a wager on a game, his enjoyment is greatly increased if he can watch or listen to it. When there is both a big increase in media coverage of games and a big increase in the number of sports books with which to place wagers, there is an enormous increase in the total amount of money wagered on college basketball. That is what has happened during the last few years.

For many fans the enjoyment of being able to watch a game and wager on it more than offsets the modest cost of doing so and is considered a great value. The cost of seeing or hearing each game via cable television or the Internet is low and the average losses from point-spread wagering on college basketball games are low.

In point-spread wagering, you typically risk $11 to win $10. If you lose, you lose your $11 wager. If you win, you get back your $11 plus $10. If you randomly place point-spread wagers on games— without doing any handicapping—you will win half your wagers and lose half your wagers. That means that half of the time you will win $10 and half of the time you will lose $11. On average you will lose $.50 on each $11 wager—4.5% of every dollar wagered.

Most people do not consider 4.5% to be a high price to pay for "action"—the entertainment value of a point-spread wager. It is about the same percentage that the house takes on each pull on a slot machine, 20% of the amount that most states take out of the parimutuel pools for horse racing and only 10% of the amount you can expect to lose by playing most state lotteries.

While losing an average of 4.5% on every wager is not particularly painful, think how enjoyable college basketball wagering would be if you could win 14.5% on every dollar wagered. Not only will your average return on each wager be increased, but you probably will be willing to place greater amounts of money at risk and win more money.

What will it take to turn an average 4.5% loss into an average 14.5% gain? As described earlier, if you simply make point-spread wagers randomly, you will win 50% of the time—five out of 10 wagers. But, if you can win 60% of the time—six out of ten wagers instead of only five—you will realize an average return of 14.5% on each dollar wagered! Converting one in five losing wagers into winning wagers is an achievable objective for most college basketball fans who are willing to invest some time handicapping games in an intelligent manner.

A 14.5% return on amounts wagered is very powerful in gaining an extremely high return on a "bankroll" – the amount of money that you are willing to lose during the season. Suppose you start with a bankroll of $1000 and during the season place 50 $110 wagers—a total of $5500 in action. If you win 60% of your wagers, at the end of the season you will have your original $1000 bankroll plus $800 in winnings—an 80% return on your initial bankroll. If you win only 50% of your point spread wagers, then you have a net loss of $250 –25% of your bankroll – and have a total of only $750 at the end of the season. There are few investments that you can make for which there is a reasonable expectation of an 80% return in a four-month period, plus an enormous amount of entertainment.

The central theme of this book is that you can increase your win rate from 50% to 60% and generate high returns on an initial bankroll by spending a modest amount of time intelligently handicapping college basketball games and placing wagers. Undeniably, there is some work that must be done. There is no fool-proof formula for picking winners. However, to win consistently it is not necessary to make college basketball handicapping a full-time job. For a fan who enjoys college basketball and who wants to know about the teams he is watching anyway, only a modest amount of extra work is needed to win consistently.

This book is comprised of four additional chapters that describe how to win consistently and gain a high return from your bankroll by wagering on college basketball.

Chapter 2: The Way Things Work. College basketball wagering is an industry that has many participants, rules and customs. It includes sports books, touts and advisors, informational websites, governmental regulatory organizations, and the media, in addition to bettors. It bears many similarities to financial markets in terms of operations and the behavior of participants. The way the college basketball market works and the behavior of its participants creates the conditions that will allow you to win consistently. By understanding "how things work" you will gain an advantage even before you begin handicapping games.

Chapter 3: Principles of College Basketball Handicapping. There are a handful of principles that are the basis for intelligently handicapping college basketball games. Each principle is explained in this chapter and then translated to the step-by-step handicapping process described in Chapter 4. By understanding the basic principles you will be more adept at applying the handicapping process, and you will be better able to deal with unusual handicapping situations.

Chapter 4: Game Handicapping—A Step-By-Step Approach. This chapter provides a step-by-step approach for handicapping a college basketball game. A special emphasis is placed on efficiency—focusing your time and effort on what is important so that a game can be effectively handicapped in about 20 minutes. The approach is applied to a game from the 2005 NCAA Men's Basketball Tournament—North Carolina State vs. UNC-Charlotte—so you can see precisely how the approach works and how to evaluate the quality of your analysis after the game has been played.

Chapter 5: Summary. This chapter summarizes the key things to always remember when wagering on college basketball. During the course of each season, there will be winning and losing streaks and emotional highs and lows. However, regardless of those conditions it is important to maintain an intelligent approach to college basketball wagering. Investing a few minutes periodically to review this chapter may help you to maintain the right perspective on wagering on college basketball.

2. The Way Things Work

To successfully wager on college basketball you must understand how things work—where betting lines come from, how sports books operate, how to manage your money and who you are wagering against. This provides a framework for understanding how you will be able to gain an advantage and win more consistently. As in most business and gaming situations, the more you understand the rules and the other participants and their motives, the easier it is to be successful.

The purpose of this chapter is to briefly describe the way things work—not to comprehensively address all aspects of wagering on college basketball. Understanding these things and acting on them will give you more confidence and provide a winning advantage even before you begin handicapping games.

1. *You are largely wagering against people like yourself who are more fans than professional sports bettors—you are not really betting against the sports book.*

Many who wager on college basketball start with a defeatist attitude: "How am I going to beat the book?" The sports book is an intimidating foe. Such gamblers expect to lose, adopt the behavior of losers, and therefore end up losing.

7

However, when the same people bet on a game with one of their friends, they are loaded with confidence and optimism. They feel confident that they can do better than someone like them.

Yet the reality is that for the most common propositions for college basketball games, and certainly point-spread wagering, you are really wagering against other people like yourself—not the sports book. This is a perspective that you must adopt.

Sports books operate very much like brokers and exchanges for other assets like stocks. They make most of their money from "making a market." They match bettors for the two sides of a proposition, rather than taking a position on one side or another. When you place a point-spread wager on a team, the sports book essentially matches your wager against someone who is interested in taking the other side of the proposition. The sports book acts more like an intermediary and clearinghouse for wagering transactions— much as your stock broker and the New York Stock Exchange.

The most common type of college basketball proposition is the point-spread wager. You can either choose Team A and get a certain number of points or Team B and give the same number of points. If Team A is favored by five points (expressed as -5), it must win the game by more than 5 points for you to win the wager. If Team B is getting five points (expressed as +5), it must lose by less than five points or win outright for you to win the wager. If Team A wins by exactly five points, it is a "push" and everyone who has wagered gets their money back—nobody wins, nobody loses.

A common business objective for sports books is to have an equal amount of money wagered on each side of a point-spread proposition. When they are successful at achieving that balance then they are assured of making money.

In point-spread propositions, a sports book typically pays out $10 in winnings for each $11 wagered on the winning side, but keeps the $11 wagered by people who have taken the losing side. If there is an equal amount wagered on both sides of a proposition, then the sports book earns 4.5% on each dollar it handles. On average, the sports book keeps $0.50 of every $11 wagered. Obviously, the more dollars wagered on the point-spread proposition, the more the sports book earns.

What this really means is that when you go to a sports book and wager $11 on Team A giving five points, the sports book is implicitly matching it to an $11 wager made by someone else on Team B getting five points. Most of the time the person who takes Team B will be someone like you who simply has a different opinion about the outcome of the game.

Therefore, to be successful in college basketball wagering, it is merely necessary to be more astute than other fans like yourself.

"Balancing the book" is an important part of operating a sports book. Sports books have systems for monitoring the cumulative amounts wagered on each side of a proposition. When there are imbalances—for example, more money wagered on Team A than Team B—the sports book adjusts the point spread to restore balance. In this situation, the sports book would move Team A to -5.5 points and Team B to +5.5 points, thereby discouraging wagering on Team A and encouraging wagering on Team B. As a practical matter, sports books cannot perfectly balance the book on a proposition, so at game time they typically have modest positions on one side or the other. To the extent that this happens and they win, the 4.5% margin increases a bit. If they lose, the margin decreases a bit. But, over the course of a season in which point-spread propositions are handled for hundreds of college basketball games, a typical sports book will seek to retain 4.5% from all money wagered.

You might think of sports books like stock exchanges and placing wagers like trading stocks. If you have a share of Microsoft that you want to sell at $25 you or your broker offer to sell it on various stock exchanges. If there is someone who wants to buy a share of Microsoft at $25, the match is made and the transaction is completed. If no one wants to buy it at $25, you might decide to reduce your price to $24.50 to attract buyers and to make the sale. When the sale is made, a small fee is paid to compensate the brokers and exchanges for having in place and operating the market to match sellers and buyers. Neither the broker nor the exchanges are buyers or sellers—they are merely intermediaries. They make money from handling the transaction. The more transactions and the more money involved in those transactions, the more they make in fees.

The idea of beating the sports book is intimidating. But to win you simply need to do better than other people much like yourself. You must adopt this perspective and wager with confidence. By putting in slightly more effort and handicapping more intelligently than your competitors you can gain a winning advantage.

2. *With a modest amount of effort you can easily outperform other bettors and consistently win.*

In point-spread wagering, you are largely wagering against other people like yourself—not the sports book. These people fall into three categories: recreational bettors, serious but inept bettors, and serious and skilled bettors.

The vast majority of point-spread bettors wager on college basketball for entertainment and recreational purposes. They enjoy the action and they consider the cost—4.5% of amounts wagered—to be modest. These bettors do not put in a lot of effort to systematically handicap games and search for the best point spreads. They can be easily beaten with only a modest effort and intelligent handicapping

A small percentage of bettors who place point-spread wagers are serious about winning. They consider placing their money at risk a form of investment—entertainment is of secondary importance. They make their decisions using data and some analysis. However, probably less than half of these bettors are truly systematic and insightful in their analysis of games, so they are unlikely to win much more than half of the time. Bettors who are serious about wagering on college basketball are not necessarily highly sophisticated and know how to take advantage of the data and analytical tools that are available. These bettors also can be beaten with only a modest amount of effort and intelligent handicapping.

Only a small proportion of the college basketball wagering public is both serious and skilled in forecasting the point spread outcomes of basketball games and capable of winning on a consistent basis. These people can be considered the professional players, "wise guys" or "smart money." Even though they place large wagers, they do not dominate point-spread wagering, particularly when there are hundreds of games that can be bet on each week.

The main thing to remember is that there is a lot more dumb money being wagered than smart money. Your hurdle for gaining an advantage and winning consistently is to be a more astute bettor than the people in the first two categories—those who are primarily interested in entertainment and those who are serious about winning but not very skilled.

By putting in some effort and doing the right analysis, you can consistently do better than the dumb money and occasionally do as well as the smart money. In doing so you can expect to achieve a 60% win rate than translates to a high return on your bankroll.

3. *Professional sports bettors play a role in college basketball wagering, but they do not dominate it.*

There are certainly people wagering on college basketball who could be considered professional sports bettors. They consider sports wagering their profession. They have much more at stake in winning than most bettors. They expend a substantial amount of effort to win and are good at it.

Professional sports bettors include syndicates that rely on computer models and individuals that have their own handicapping systems. Even with a broad definition of "professional," there are few people who are sufficiently skilled in wagering on college basketball games and other sports that they can make a living doing it. There are several reasons for this.

First, only the successful survive—there is a Darwinian process in sports wagering. Those who can't consistently win must move on to other professions. Second, professional sports wagering is hard work—handicapping games takes analytical expertise and skills in manipulating and interpreting data. There are many more people that would like to be professional bettors than are capable of it because they lack either the skills or discipline to do so. Third, many of the same skills that it takes to be a successful professional sports bettor can be more profitably applied in other professions. Fourth, it is hard to make a healthy living without placing large wagers and putting lots of money at risk. Many people simply do not have the capital to do so and others cannot afford large, short-term losses that periodically occur for even the most skilled and sophisticated bettor.

The difficulty of making a healthy living from sports wagering is the reason why there are so many people who assert that they are professional handicappers and want to *sell* you their picks": their pick of the hour, their pick of the week, their pick of the season, their pick of the century and so on. There are dozens of "advisors" who would like to sell you their picks on a game-by-game basis or on a full-season subscription. Many professional sports bettors figure that once they have already done the hard work of handicapping a game, the extra cost of selling the results to others is very low, while the revenue can be significant.

Handicapping college basketball games and placing large wagers on them entails risk—some days you win big, some days you lose big. However, if you are selling your advice, you can win every day. It is risk-free income. Income from selling advice combined with winnings from placing their own bets is what enables many people to earn enough money to be professional sports bettors.

Professional sports bettors affect but do not dominate college basketball wagering. They try to do what you will be trying to do—

spot big differences in the point spread relative to the likely outcome of a game. When they spot differences they will wager on the side that has been undervalued by the betting public. As they do so, and money flows to the undervalued side, the point spread is diminished, making it less undervalued for other bettors.

There is still plenty of room for the individual college basketball handicapper to find very good wagering opportunities and to consistently win. Remember, the majority of your competition consists of people wagering largely for entertainment purposes and/or those without a significant level of handicapping skill. Also, there are hundreds of college basketball games during each week of the season. Professional bettors, as a group, cannot fully evaluate each game and wager enough money to eliminate all advantages relative to the point spread in every game. Sometimes you will be wagering on games of great interest to professionals and at other times you will not. Even in games that are of interest to professionals, you may find an advantage in a game and place your wager before "smart money" begins to move the point spread. As will be discussed later, offshore sports books level the playing field for all bettors—professional and amateur—with respect to the terms of point spread propositions and the timing of wagers.

To better understand why wagering on college basketball represents a good opportunity to be entertained and make money, compare it to trading stocks on the New York Stock Exchange. Almost everyone who invests in stocks does so to win—to make money. There are not many people who buy stocks for entertainment purposes--so that they can sit in front of their computers all day watching the prices fluctuate! Because the capitalization of publicly traded companies is so great there is an enormous amount of money to be made or lost in trading stocks.

Not surprisingly, trading stocks attracts the most sophisticated institutions staffed by some of the most sophisticated stock research and trading professionals whose extremely healthy compensation depends on their winning more than losing. While there are millions of Americans who own stocks, professionals dominate the stock markets. The majority of trades each day are made by or for investing professionals. These professionals are armed with more extensive data and more extensive research than the general investing public. It is hard for individuals to successfully compete with professionals in trading the stock of public companies.

The virtue of betting on college basketball is that you don't have to consistently beat professionals to be very successful. In college basketball wagering there are professionals who will do better than you, but they don't dominate the market and squeeze out the advantage that can be achieved by well-prepared individual bettors. If you do your homework, there is no reason to be intimidated by professionals. You should feel confident about your ability to win.

4. *Under certain circumstances it may be desirable to buy advice—but be cautious!*

A common question is: "Handicapping takes some work—isn't it easier and just as effective to buy advice from professional college basketball handicappers who do it for a living?"

The most common answer given is: "If these people are so smart and can win so often, why are they in the business of selling picks?" As described above, even those professionals who win more than they lose can supplement their income by selling advice.

There is no doubt that some professional handicappers sell very good advice. The problem is figuring out which ones. The sports handicapping industry has a poor reputation that is perpetuated by unbelievable claims, exaggerated chest thumping, and a high decibel level. Handicappers selling picks have found that marketing, sales and various customer retention techniques are more important for generating revenue than the quality of their picks.

You might look at college basketball advisory services as you would a financial advisor or stockbroker. There is nothing inherently wrong with gaining high quality professional help. If you can find someone who can consistently give you good advice so that you win

60% of your wagers, then that is a valuable source of assistance. It might be preferable to buy advice rather than to go to the effort of doing your own handicapping.

The problem is how to determine who provides consistently reliable winning advice and whether it is worth paying for. Because picks are only made available to people who pay for them, it is hard to know what a handicapper's actual win rate has been. While there are now some services that claim they rate the handicapping services and monitor their win rates, they rarely reveal how they do it. Also, many of the win rates seem implausibly high and there are suspected conflicts of interest between the rating services and the handicappers.

The other thing about handicapping services is that they focus more on what the pick is rather than why it is the right pick. Professional handicappers provide relatively little analysis to justify their conclusions, and what little they do provide is relatively superficial. It is very hard for you to evaluate a pick until the game is actually played. Even then, you may find it hard to determine whether it was a winner or loser because of analysis or luck.

You might consider buying advice from a handicapping service if three criteria are met:

- *Justification of picks.* If you ask your broker why she is recommending a specific stock, she will give you the report prepared by the research division of her brokerage firm. You can determine if the analysis seems to make sense before buying the stock. Similarly, a college basketball advisory service that provides a detailed analysis and complete justification for its picks offers similar value. You will feel more confident when you follow its advice and, of course, if a particular pick doesn't seem to be justified, you have the opportunity to refrain from betting.

- *Specialization in college basketball.* All handicapping services claim excellent results. So you must try to sort through all of the claims and ascertain which ones seem plausible. If you are interested in wagering on college basketball, then you are interested in how well a handicapping service does on its college basketball picks. It doesn't matter how well the service does on football or baseball. There is power in specialization—you wouldn't have brain surgery done by a general practitioner. In general, handicappers who specialize in basketball rather than trying to cover most sports will be more successful. If their financial success depends on basketball, that provides a powerful incentive to pick winners.

- *Cost of advice.* Depending on the amount of your average wager, the cost of advice can more than offset your additional winnings. For example, if you must pay $20 for each pick, then to break even during the season your average wager should be $120 and you should be able to move from a 50% unit win rate to a 60% unit win rate. The conundrum is that most bettors who are not trying to get rich from college basketball wagering do not bet sufficient amounts to cover the cost of advice—even if it is good advice.

5. ***There are many types of college basketball wagering propositions, but the traditional point-spread wager still provides the best opportunity for most bettors.***

The point spread proposition has been the core of college basketball wagering for decades. It is still the most pervasive proposition—the one you will see at every sports book and addressed by almost every handicapper, advisor and tout. It is still the proposition that provides the best opportunity for most betters interested in both entertainment and winning.

In the last few years, sports book have come up with many new types of propositions. The objective of all sports books has been to respond to the desires of the wagering public by emulating the diverse propositions of NFL games--which attract the most wagering—and thereby increase the total amount wagered on college basketball.

Some sports books have created new propositions to differentiate themselves from their competitors.

For example, it is now common to wager on college basketball teams to win games outright and to wager on the total points scored for the game and in each half. It is possible to place futures bets—wagering on a team to win a conference championship or tournament. In the last year or so, it has become possible to place over/under wagers on such things as three point shots made, rebounds and turnovers in NCAA tournament games.

Sports books also offer many new variations on traditional point-spread wagers. It is commonly possible to make point-spread wagers on the first and second halves, as well as the entire game. It is now possible to buy or sell points—for example, to accept a lower winning payoff in return for getting more points. For some games, there is now an interactive real-time market in which it is possible to place a wager and lock in a point spread, and then to sell your bet to others during the course of the game. With the ebb and flow of the game the value of your point spread position will fluctuate, and of course the sports book is always happy to match buyers and sellers who can agree on a price as long as it results in more transactions and fees.

The primary reasons why the types of propositions have increased has important consequences for those who wager. In most cases, they provide more benefit to the sports book than to members of the wagering public who are as interested in winning as being entertained.

Many argue that sports books are simply meeting the demand of the wagering public. The number of types of propositions has increased in every other major sport over the last few years, so the wagering public is seeking and receptive to more ways to play. If the public wants more college basketball propositions, then sports books are happy to accommodate them. The extra operating cost that a sports book incurs when it adds more propositions is fairly low, and the potential increase in profit is high.

The sports wagering business is highly competitive. There are now more than 100 offshore sports books in addition to the dozens in Nevada. All sports books offer the same basic point-spread propositions and very similar point spreads. Many sports books try to differentiate themselves from the others based on the propositions they offer. They try to offer more propositions than other sports books in hopes of becoming the preferred sports book of many bettors—the sports book that a bettor opens an account with and goes to first when considering placing a wager.

In expanding the types of propositions offered, sports books have turned a potential problem into an opportunity. The potential problem with many of the new and novel propositions is that it is hard to balance the book—to get an equal amount wagered on each side of a proposition. Sports books are not as adept at setting reliable opening lines on these propositions that anticipate the perspective of the betting public. The closing lines frequently are different than opening lines. Also, because some of the propositions and do not draw large numbers of bettors or amounts wagered, sports books cannot change the lines quickly enough to reliably balance the book.

In handling these propositions, sports books incur a greater risk of an unbalanced book which results in holding a position counter to the majority of the wagering public on many propositions. While there may be times when a sports book wants to take a position on a proposition, it does not want to do so regularly and to have the position it takes dictated by the betting public. Therefore, sports books make the best of this situation by charging a higher transaction fee for these types of wagers. They pass through the cost of their increased financial risk to those placing the wagers.

Consider the case in which you wager on a team to win a college basketball game outright. Ironically, betting on a team to win a game seems like the most obvious type of wager to place, yet traditionally this type of college basketball proposition has not been consistently offered by sports books. If we continue with the example above,

Teams A and B are competitive but Team A, favored by five points, is considered the better team and more likely to win.

In this case, the moneyline on Team A to win might be -350, while the moneyline for Team B to win might be +250. That means you must wager $350 to win $100 if Team A wins; and if you wager $100 on Team B, you will win $250 if it wins.

If the book is balanced in terms of amounts wagered on each side of the proposition, what is the outcome for the sports book? Say $100 is wagered on each team. If Team A actually wins, then the sports book returns the $100 wagered plus $28.58 in winnings. However, the sports book will keep the $100 wagered on Team B. That means that overall the sports book will net $71.42 from the wagers on this game.

Conversely, if Team B wins the book must return the $100 wagered, plus pay out $250 in winnings. However, it will retain the $100 wagered on Team A. In this situation, its net loss will be $150.

As a result, the sports book will win or lose money on each college basketball game for which this type of proposition is handled. It will try to set the differences in moneylines as wide as the wagering public will allow with the idea of winning more when it wins and losing less when it loses.

While the example has substantial differences in outcomes for the sports book—winning $71.42 or losing $150—you must remember that Team A is the favorite and Team B is the underdog. Therefore, Team A, as a five point favorite, is approximately twice as likely to win as Team B. Therefore, the expected winnings when Team A wins are $71.42 and the expected losses from Team B winning are about $75.00 ($150 x 50%).

On a Saturday afternoon during the college basketball season, the sports book will handle this proposition for dozens of games. It will win money on some and lose money on others. On most

Saturdays it will win more than it loses, but there are Saturdays when it loses more than it wins. In return for accepting more risk in this type of proposition, the sports book builds in higher commissions—basically increasing the spread between what it wins if it wins and what it loses if it loses. These implicit fees are always higher than the 4.5% cost to play on traditional point spread propositions.

What does this mean in terms of how you wager? The higher the transaction fees—i.e., the percentage of amounts bet retained by the sports book—the harder it is to be a cumulative winner over an entire season. The higher the fees, the higher the percentage of wagers that you need to win to simply break even. For traditional point-spread propositions you only need to win about 52.25% of your wagers to break even. However, for more novel types of propositions, with much higher risk-based transaction fees built into the proposition, you need to win more frequently and/or win at longer odds.

It is only desirable to wager on these propositions if you specialize in one or more of them and can gain a sufficient advantage to overcome the higher transaction costs. Despite the bigger cut taken by the sports books, you are still largely wagering against other individuals. On average, the amounts wagered on these types of propositions are based on a lot of emotion and somewhat less analysis than traditional point-spread propositions. Most bettors simply don't know how to forecast many of the outcomes that are addressed by more novel propositions and aren't able to as finely discriminate good odds or moneylines from bad ones. Therefore, you can gain a consistent advantage on propositions other than point spreads, but you will have to make a serious commitment to college basketball handicapping, in terms of both time spent and effort expended. That is why the handicapping principles and process described in Chapters 3 and 4 focus on traditional point-spread wagers—the type of proposition that best balances the time you need to spend handicapping, your potential to win money, and your entertainment from watching and wagering on games.

6. *An advantage is gained by specializing in specific types of propositions*

Your source of advantage in college basketball wagering, as in most sports wagering, is to be more skillful than most of the betting public in forecasting what will happen in specific games. The advantage is converted to winnings when you find propositions for which the terms do not reflect the forecasted results of the game and you bet on the side of the proposition that is undervalued.

An advantage can be gained in any type of college basketball wagering proposition, not only point-spread propositions. However, to do so you must specialize in specific types of propositions—invest time and effort to become truly expert in those types of propositions. As described in Subsection 5, specialization enables you to gain a sufficient advantage to offset the transaction fees collected by the sports book and to earn a higher win rate that most other bettors against whom you are competing.

The power of specialization is realized in four ways.

First, only by specializing can you discover the valid cause and effect relationships that enable you to forecast game outcomes that, in turn, provide you with the chance to spot miss-priced propositions. For example, the relationships that will enable you to forecast the total points that will be scored in a game so that you can wager on the over/under of point totals are different than the relationships that will enable you to figure out what the margin of victory will be so that you can wager on a game's point-spread proposition.

Second, there are too many propositions for each game to easily analyze in order to find good wagering opportunities. To fully analyze all of the propositions that are offered for a single major college basketball game could take an entire day, and you still might not find any propositions that are advantageous. Since you only have a limited amount of time to allocate to handicapping each game, it is important to be focused on specific propositions.

Third, different propositions require different types of data for analysis. If you were to try to evaluate all propositions for a game, the data collection and manipulation task would be enormous. You would be trying to collect, manipulate and use virtually all of the data that is available for the two teams playing the game. Such a large data management effort is prohibitive for the person who wants to win, but not make the analysis of basketball games their life's work.

Fourth, there is an important benefit from the repetition of considering a specific type of proposition. You will quickly identify certain patterns in the way terms are set and sports books that tend to offer the best terms. You will quickly identify the patterns and tendencies of teams that have the most bearing on outcomes. You will be able to handicap more efficiently--either covering more ground in the time you allocate to handicapping or reducing the time it takes you to conduct specific analyses.

There are several other considerations that have a bearing on the specific types of propositions in which you choose to specialize. While it is possible to be successful wagering on any type of proposition, the traditional point-spread proposition is probably the one that you should favor.

The ability to win is based on your knowledge and forecasting skills relative to other bettors. It is sometimes possible to more easily gain an advantage in less common or interesting propositions. For example, perhaps only a small percentage of bettors on point totals (over/under) are really serious about it—suppose that most are simply playing hunches. If that is the case, a specialization in over/under wagers could be quite profitable.

At the same time, you are placing wagers to increase your satisfaction from watching or listening to the game, having some action on the game, and winning more often than you lose. Some types of propositions, while perhaps offering a better chance to win, may not enhance your enjoyment of watching the game or having some action. Continuing with the example above, you can probably find a way to have a high win rate for over/under wagers. However, if you are like most college basketball fans, those wagers are not likely to enhance your enjoyment in watching games. Playing an "under" on a game's total score and spending the entire game rooting for both teams to miss shots is not most fans' idea of a good time!

Another consideration is money management. In point-spread wagering it is uncommon to go on long losing or winning streaks. As long as the random chances of winning are in the range of 50%, the chances of losing five straight point-spread wagers is only less than 4%--regardless of whether you wager on favorites or underdogs.

However, if you are wagering on teams to win outright there is a greater variance in outcomes. You can go for a while without winning and then have reasonably large wins. Conversely, you can win small amounts consistently and then lose those winnings quickly. In contrast to point-spread wagers, if you were to wager on a 2-1 underdog to win five consecutive times, the chances of losing all of those wagers is 13.2%. What this means is that for most propositions other than point spreads, there are wider swings in the value of your bankroll. It becomes important to avoid the propositions that have a material risk of wiping out your entire bankroll early in the season unless you are very sure that you can gain a large advantage from specializing.

In summary, it is possible to gain an advantage by specializing in any of the common college basketball wagering propositions. However, college basketball fans who desire to increase their wagering win rate should start out by specializing in point-spread wagering. Point-spread wagering offers the advantages of low fees to sports books, low risk of losing your bankroll early, easy to apply techniques for game analysis, readily available data to support your analysis, and high entertainment value.

It is for these reasons that point-spread wagering is the focus of this book.

7. College basketball wagering has a high level of integrity— much higher than in the days of the local bookie.

The reputation of college basketball has been tarnished because of gambling. There have been several well-publicized cases of game fixing and point shaving. However, most of those incidents are in the distant past—some more than 50 years ago! Today, the overall level of integrity of wagering on college basketball is arguably as high as trading stocks, bonds, real estate, art and other types of assets.

The fundamental reason for a high level of integrity in college basketball wagering is that there are so many constituencies that have a vested interest in a clean game. The NCAA is very vigilant in maintaining the integrity of the sport through its education, surveillance and investigation programs. College administrators are more vigilant than ever before because of the potentially high cost of a gambling scandal—in terms of the prestige and reputation of the university and, of course, potentially large losses of revenue from boosters and tournament payouts. Coaches are more vigilant than ever before because, while they have more pressure to win, they are compensated at extraordinary levels that they are very unlikely to knowingly jeopardize. Sports books are more vigilant than ever. More than fearing a one-time loss from a fixed game, they fear a scandal that could sharply curtail the level of sports wagering and, also, provide ammunition to the proponents of legislation to ban wagering on college sports. In fact, in the few recent cases of point shaving in college basketball, it was sports books that first detected irregularities and alerted federal authorities. Finally, now there are also foreign governments that are vitally interested in the integrity of American sports events since some smaller countries in the Caribbean and Central America rely on offshore gaming as a significant part of their economies. A sharp reduction in gaming and sports wagering would create unemployment problems and diminished tax revenues.

In addition to all of these deterrents, the plain fact is that there are much more desirable opportunities for illegal activity than fixing college basketball games. There are many opportunities for illegal activity in which there are not so many organizations acting as watchdogs, where the outcome of one's illegal actions can be more certain and the upside can be higher, and where the crime is deemed a state or local matter rather than a federal matter.

Finally, when we compare the integrity of wagering on college basketball to the integrity of trading stocks, bonds, art and other asset classes, the former does not suffer. Despite federal and state watchdogs and stringent public and regulatory reporting requirements, there are some publicly traded companies that have experienced malfeasance that has been very costly to their stockholders. It might be argued that the cases of insider trading of publicly traded companies are akin to fixing college basketball games. It might be argued that the average bettor on college basketball has access to a higher percentage of relevant information on which to make their wagering decisions than investors in public companies. Public companies make available a small fraction of the information that has a bearing on their earnings; it is hard to imagine data on most college basketball teams that is not available. It might be argued that wagering on college basketball is not nearly as susceptible to fraud as dealing in art or collectibles.

In summary, while college basketball wagering may have a bit of a tarnished past, it now looks and operates a lot like the markets for more conventional assets and has as much integrity.

8. The expansion of wagering on college basketball in Nevada and offshore is driving the local bookie out of business.

For years wagering on college basketball was done through local bookies. Bettors had little information on which to base their wagers. They couldn't shop among bookies for the best terms. They had little recourse if their bookie decided not to pay off or left town with their money. They paid a very high vigorish (transaction fee) to the bookie to reflect his risk of arrest, fines and jail time. Bookies were running a black market and those that chose to wager with them had no choice but to do it under the terms that the bookies dictated.

Today, hundreds of offshore sports books constitute a transparent market. In contrast to local bookies that run a "black market," these sports books constitute a "white market." Propositions and terms offered by each sports book can be easily identified and compared. The vigorish is driven down by competition among sports books as well as diminishing operating costs. Finally, in most cases, funds are secure the payout of winnings is very reliable.

Financial integrity is critical to the sports wagering industry as well as every sports book. Sports book operators ensure financial integrity to maintain the viability of their businesses. Because there are so many offshore sports books from which to chose, there is no reason to create or maintain an account with a sports book for which there is any question about financial integrity. Sports books are very fearful of churn—losing customers to competitors. Sports books work hard to keep you as a customer and they know that without financial integrity all other efforts are useless.

Sports books in Nevada have been regulated for many years. Offshore sports books that constitute an important part of some local economies in the Caribbean and Central America are increasingly regulated. Some foreign governments license sports books and provide minimum assurances of solvency.

The consequences of breeches of financial integrity are swift and severe. There is a strong grassroots consumer protection network. Word travels quickly about sports books that do not pay promptly or cannot be relied on to book the right bets or maintain accurate accounts. In fact, there are websites that rate offshore sports books and/or consolidate feedback from bettors in addition to dozens of message boards related to sports wagering.

With the pervasiveness of the Internet and proliferation of offshore sports books, the local bookie has been greatly affected in two ways. First, the sports wagering handle of bookies has decreased. Today, the only advantage that the local bookie can offer to the sports bettor that might in any way offset the many disadvantages is credit and the ability to place impulse bets. Fortunately, most people who bet on college basketball do not need or desire to wager on credit—which is never a good idea. Also, while a bettor must set up an account with an offshore sports book, it is a modest effort for anyone who intends to wager on college basketball during the course of a season and who desires to avoid all of the disadvantages of dealing with a bookie.

Second, a local bookie who continues to handle sports wagering will be kept more honest by the offshore sports books. Even if you choose to place wagers with a bookie, it is now easy to determine what the prevailing terms for each type of proposition are by checking any of the many websites that provide such information on a very timely basis. More than in the past, local bookies are dealing with more informed consumers and must set the terms of propositions to largely reflect those that exist in Las Vegas and offshore books. Matching those terms reduces the profit margins of bookies and increases their risk, since unlike the offshore books they probably do not have enough customers to consistently balance the book. Over time, bookies will find that they are in the unsecured short-term loan business as much as the sports wagering business and turn their attention to other activities.

9. Accounts with offshore sports books are required unless you plan to move to Las Vegas or do business with local bookies

There are currently more than 100 offshore sports books from which to choose—although there are actually fewer choices than it may appear. It is reasonably common for several sports books to be operated by the same organization using the same technology infrastructure and information systems. The things that are different are the names of the books, the parts of their websites that are visible to bettors, and the approaches that they adopt to appeal to specific parts of the sports wagering public. However, this is actually not too much different than the brokerage industry. More than a few discount brokers actually execute trades through larger brokers that have a more extensive infrastructure and more sophisticated trading systems.

Nevertheless, there is now a lot of competition among offshore sports books that works to the benefit of those who wager on college basketball. Sports books badly want your business and as each new college basketball season comes along they introduce new services and incentives to attract and retain you as a customer. While you will be offered many inducements by sports books, the key attributes of the type of sports book you should deal with are described in Subsection 9.

Unless you are going to move to Nevada or prefer to deal with a local bookie, you will need an account with one or more offshore sports books. Your account will work like a brokerage account. You will make cash deposits that will be credited to your account. When you place wagers, funds will be withdrawn and applied to your wager. If you win, your original bet and winnings will be credited to your account. You can check your account each day to see the current account balance, the outcome and settlement on prior wagers, and the pending wagers.

Opening an account is easy; funding it is a little more difficult. New accounts can be opened at every sports book's website in a matter of minutes. However, in much the same way as a bank account, the account is not operative until funds are deposited. In the recent past it was possible to simply use a major credit card to fund an account. Rather than address the issue of legality head on, the U.S. government has taken various indirect actions to restrain trade in offshore sports books and gambling. Recently, major credit card companies, under pressure from government agencies, have declined to allow sports books to act as merchants. Most credit cards can no longer be used to fund offshore sports book accounts.

There are two very common methods for funding accounts. First, bank wires can be used to move funds from your bank to the sports book through the international banking network. This is a very safe process that is used daily for billions of dollars of international transactions. Typically, the transfer of funds can be completed in three to five business days.

Second, you can use a payment intermediary like NETELLER or PayPal. You can easily create accounts with those organizations and then use a credit card or electronic check to fund them. They, in turn, use the money in your account with them to pay Internet merchants or others as you direct them to do so. Funds that are placed in one of these intermediary accounts can be transferred to offshore sport book accounts within a few minutes.

Withdrawing funds from an account is not difficult. Sports books will typically transfer funds to you in whatever manner you prefer, typically through the same means as deposits have been made. Most are extremely diligent in transferring funds. Sports books fully understand that, more than almost any other factor, its integrity in the eyes of the betting public depends on how quickly it pays off— that is, how quickly and easily an account holder can get money from his account. The fastest way to lose customers is unreasonable delays in transferring funds.

10. All sports books are not the same—open accounts with those that help you gain a tangible advantage.

You will need an account with at least one sports book, but it is desirable to have accounts with two or three sports books. Many people think that the reason for doing so is to avoid the risk of sports books going out of business or simply disappearing with your money. There was probably a time when that was a good reason for multiple accounts. While that might be a minor reason for doing so today, there are many more compelling reasons that provide you a winning advantage. There is a sound dollars and cents justification for multiple accounts that more than offsets the extra effort of setting up additional accounts.

There are three material ways that sports books differ that can work to your benefit. It is important to identify those reputable sports books that separately and in combination provide tangible benefits that you, in fact, will realize. A common marketing tool of sports books is to offer services or benefits that you will never be able to use or, if you do, will cost more than they are worth. While comparing sports books is not nearly as difficult as comparing the plans of cellular carriers or insurance companies, you will get a high payoff from the effort you expend in doing so.

The standard point-spread moneyline has been and continues to be -110—putting $11 at risk to win $10. As noted earlier, when a sports book is successful in "balancing the book" it can count on about a 4.5% risk fee return on money wagered. However, because of increasing competition, some sports books are choosing to essentially cut their prices to gain business. They are willing to reduce the moneyline and their risk-free return to attract more accounts and stimulate greater levels of wagering.

They do this in several different ways, but the benefits are clear. If the transaction cost—the expected amount that goes to the sports book for providing the market and handling the transaction—goes down, your wagering dollars go farther and your expected net winnings are greater. When you win, you win the same amount; but when you lose, you lose less.

With the traditional moneyline of -110, on average, you will get back 95.5% of the money you place at risk—slightly less than the return from a flip of a coin. However, if a sports book cuts the moneyline in half to -105—risking $10.50 to win $10—on average you will get back 97.75% of the money placed at risk. That might not seem like much, but if you are trying get back 110% of every dollar wagered—a healthy winning margin—it gets you 15.5% of the way there without requiring you to improve your handicapping skills or the frequency with which you win.

There are several ways in which sports books discount the vigorish. The most straightforward way is to simply modify the traditional moneyline—making it lower for all point-spread propositions.

An alternative that is becoming more popular is a bit more complex. When the book opens, it will establish a point-spread for a game and a balanced moneyline (-110; +110). The sports book will never alter the point spread. However, as it takes money it will vary the moneyline to represent the preferences of the wagering public. When a disproportionate amount of money flows to one side of a proposition, the sports book simply increases the moneyline on that side and lowers it on the other. In the former case, the payoff for covering is lowered; in the latter case, it is increased. This is the mechanism by which the sports book changes the incentives to wager on each side of a proposition and to move towards a risk-adjusted balanced book. However, the closing point spread will be the same as the opening point spread, but the closing moneylines may be a different from the opening moneylines.

Another common arrangement is to offer discounts on certain days of the week or on specific games. The sports books try to induce bettors to check their websites frequently to see if there are "specials" that they can take advantage of, and to entice bettors to wager on days that there are relatively few games on the board and the overall level of action is expected to be low. In fact, during football season, Tuesdays are a common day in which discounts and other inducements are offered. In general, searching for these types of discounts is more trouble than it is worth unless you find books that reliably offer them week after week.

Many sports books offer affinity programs. Similar to airline frequent flyer programs and casino comps, sports books offer premiums to account holders who place significant funds at risk. However, in general, the value of these premiums is relatively low and the cost, in terms of risking more funds than might be wise, can be high. In the same way that some people fly more than they need, take flights with stops, or pay higher fares in order to get frequent flyer miles, bettors are susceptible to accepting propositions that have terms that are worse than the rest of the market in order to gain credits in the sports book's affinity program. In general, affinity programs should be ignored when you select a sports book.

The second attribute that differentiates sports books is the propositions that they handle and the consistency with which they handle them. In general, the larger the sports book, the more comprehensive the propositions it offers. The reason, of course, is that it has enough account holders to generate action on the various propositions to make handling them worthwhile. Also, it can bear the additional risk of propositions for which it is difficult to balance the book.

It is important that you maintain accounts with sports books that comprehensively and consistently handle the types of college basketball propositions that you specialize in. To the extent that you specialize in more conventional point-spread propositions then the offerings of all sports books are essentially the same. Remember the things that are most important in selecting a sports book with which to do business concern college basketball—their capabilities and policies regarding football, baseball, hockey and other sports are immaterial.

The third major differentiator among sports books that can provide you with a material advantage is how early they begin accepting wagers for college basketball games. If you are a person who does his homework ahead of time—a day in advance of the game—then a sports book that takes money the night before game day is very valuable.

The source of this value is that when point spreads are first posted they are most likely to be mis-priced—that is, to vary from the perceptions of the betting public regarding game outcomes. Invariably, the final point spread on a game is different than the first spread posted. As mentioned earlier, sports books adjust the point spread to reflect the wagers that are placed. It is not uncommon for the point spread to change by several points as the market adjusts prior to game time.

If you have done your homework early and analyzed a game you will have a better chance of exploiting an imperfection in an opening line. You will frequently be able to gain a point spread the night before the game that is very favorable relative to your forecast of the game outcome that will not be available later. Over the course of the following 24 hours others in the market may see the same things as you see and the point spread will become less favorable. It may not always be desirable to place a wager early, but it is valuable to deal with a sports book that consistently provides you with the option to do so.

This can become a powerful advantage. Suppose it makes the difference between losing and winning 5% of the time, or once in every 20 games. That is a big swing towards your goal of winning 60% of the time.

Sports books that take money the night before the game absorb more risk but offer bettors that do their homework early additional value. The majority of sports books post lines and take money on game day once they think that the lines have largely settled and that there will not be too much further adjustment that would make it difficult to balance the book. In many respects this is similar to other commodity markets in which there are essentially a few firms or brokers that are "price setters" and the vast majority are "price followers."

The discussion thus far has addressed the considerations in selecting a single sports book with which to do business. As important are the benefits from having accounts with several sports books.

Even though there is some extra effort to set up and monitor multiple accounts, it is worth doing so. While point spreads for a college basketball game are very similar among sports books, they are not always identical. Sports books balance their books based on the wagers they receive. There will be some differences in betting patterns among sports books and, therefore, the point spreads will be slightly different. The final point spread for a game will rarely be more than half a point different from one sports book to the next.

The advantage of having accounts with multiple sports books is the ability to "shop for spreads." You have the ability to compare the point spreads that the books offer and place your wager at the one which is most advantageous. You will be looking for an extra half point for your side of the point spread proposition. But, even if you cannot find an extra half point, you still may be able to find a more attractive moneyline. Sometimes placing a wager with a moneyline of -105 rather than -110 is more valuable than getting the extra half point.

Gaining an extra half point is a lot more important than it may appear. As will be discussed in Chapter 3, it is generally not desirable to wager on games in which the point spread is greater than 10. Suppose that, on average, the point spread is five in the games on which you wager. On average, every time that you get an extra half point, it is like getting an extra 10% margin for victory. Over the course of a season, this provides a real advantage and will help move your win rate towards 60%.

In summary, selection and use of sports books can create a sizable advantage for you, regardless of the handicapping methodology that you apply. The process of shopping for favorable moneylines and point spreads at sports books that begin taking money the night before the game provides an opportunity to increase your win rate to at least 55% and, on average, a positive return from each dollar wagered.

This means that the wagering process can get you half way to your win rate goal of 60%. It is not too hard to imagine a superior handicapping methodology easily getting you the rest of the way there.

11. A relatively modest bankroll can go a long way and generate a high return.

The most basic principle regarding bankrolls is that your bankroll should never be more than you can afford to lose. While no one likes to lose, a fear of losing can take much of the enjoyment out of wagering. Also, the focus and intensity that might accompany such fear does not necessarily translate into more success.

At the beginning of the season you should set your bankroll—either monthly or for the entire season. In addition to the primary criterion—risking no more than you can afford to lose—it is important to figure out the approximate amount that you would like to wager on a game to make it entertaining.

The amount that it takes to make a game entertaining is a very personal decision. Many people are happy betting only a few dollars. They get as much enjoyment from "being right" as from the amount that they win. For others it is only entertaining if the dollars at risk are material, and by consistently winning there is some extra money that can be used to buy luxuries. The more you like to wager per game the greater your bankroll must be.

However, the good news is that if you specialize in point-spread propositions your bankroll can go a long way. Suppose you have a bankroll of $100 and your average wager is $11 per game. If you choose the side on which to wager on a random basis—by flipping a coin—you will be right 50% of the time and, on average, get back $10.50 for every $11 wagered—an average loss of $.50 per game. At that rate, it will take a long time before you lose all of your money. Of course, you might encounter a run of bad luck in which you lose time after time. However, the probability of losing so consistently as to wipe out your initial bankroll of $100 in a short period of time is very low.

The better news is that if you put in the effort to gain better than random results—for example, winning three out of five games (60%)—you not only get a lot of entertainment and win some money, but your investment in college basketball becomes the best performing part of your financial portfolio!

Assume the same $100 bankroll and wagers of $11. If you win at a 60% rate, the average winnings per wager are $1.60. To work through the math, for each 10 wagers you would lose $44 and win $60—a net profit of $16. Under these circumstances you might say to yourself, "On average, every time I place $11 at risk my profit is $1.60—14.5% is a pretty good return."

The truly intoxicating thing is that the 14.5% return can occur overnight. The next day you can take the same $11 and use it again to generate 14.5%. While some days there will be winners and other days there will be losers, on average you can gain 14.5% per game. If you place one $11 wager a day for the 100 days of a basketball season, your total winning would be $160, plus your original bankroll—a return on your original bankroll of 160% in slightly more than three months!

It is for this reason that college basketball is actually a very good investment for people who are fans and are inclined to wager for entertainment anyway. There is no reason why entertainment can't also be highly profitable.

Compare this investing model—using the same funds over and over again during the course of the college basketball season—to most other asset classes. For stocks, bonds, real estate and fine art you might be happy to have a 10% annual return on investment but your money is tied up in the asset for the entire year. Certainly, there are times when higher gains are realized by buying and selling traditional assets over short periods of time, but that is more the exception than the rule.

Investing in College Basketball, a companion to this volume, demonstrates that when college basketball fans approach wagering on the sport with the same level of dedication, discipline, intensity and analysis as they apply for more traditional assets classes, the return on investment is much higher than for those asset classes.

By specializing in the teams in a specific conference throughout the season and investing 15-20 hours per week in analyzing games, it is possible to achieve a very high unit win rate (greater than 65%) that translates to a very high return on money placed at risk ($2.65 on each $11 placed at risk), which in turn translates into an extraordinary return on an original bankroll.

It is important to add a cautionary note. There is the temptation to look at these numbers and conclude that winning is a sure thing—

that if you wagered $1,100 per game rather than $11 you could get rich in a single season. There is no doubt that there is an opportunity to make a lot of money this way. However, these numbers cannot be infinitely extrapolated. It reaches the point where there are simply not enough good games to wager on to maintain a 60% win rate or that you reach wagering limits at certain sports books. These will not be constraints for the fan who wants entertainment and to win consistently, but is not trying to get rich from wagering on college basketball.

12. You can take advantage of the psychology of the wagering public.

Psychology plays a big role in wagering on college basketball. It affects the way lines are made, the way your competitors bet, and the way that you bet and manage your money. This section addresses the psychology of others and how to take advantage of it. The next section addresses your psychology and how to avoid being victimized by it.

There are plenty of opportunities for winning point-spread wagers. While there are some variations by conference and stage of the season, the average variance between game outcomes and final point spreads is typically seven to 10 points. Major conferences with the best players demonstrate more consistency and attract the most handicapping and wagering attention so the variance tends to be towards the low end. Conversely, teams in lesser conferences demonstrate more inconsistency of play and attract fewer of the best handicappers.

The final point spread on a college basketball game represents the consensus of the wagering public. Regardless of what the opening line may have been, the final line represents the dollar voting by the wagering public.

There are some key factors that influence the consensus of the wagering public. Sometimes these factors lead the public in the wrong direction. That can be bad for them, but good for you.

In the sports wagering industry, there are a handful of line makers who set the opening point spread for a game. In setting the opening point spread the line makers are projecting what the point spread should be to generate equal dollars wagered on each side of the proposition. For example, some line makers start by figuring out what the outcome of the game is likely to be and then make adjustments to those point spreads to reflect known wagering tendencies of the public.

For example, there are certain "public teams" that have sterling reputations and strong national followings. These teams always attract more wagers, particularly among those wagering strictly for entertainment. Currently, Duke and Kentucky might be considered public teams. It is reasonable to set an opening line to reflect this type of tendency.

The psychology of the general wagering public provides you with two potential advantages—unless, of course, you fall into the same traps.

The pervasiveness of power ratings has a major impact on wagering patterns in college basketball. The underlying concept is that the "power" of a team can be represented by a single number and that that number, relative to the number assigned to other teams, can be used as a reliable predictor of game outcomes.

The power ratings give casual bettors the illusion that they have the ability to easily determine the outcomes of games. Many believe that a few easy calculations will give them a good idea of the expected outcomes of games and guide them towards the right side of a point spread proposition. As a result wagering seems more accessible to anyone with a casual interest in college basketball and any of the many publicly available power ratings.

The power rating effect tends to move lines towards point spreads calculated by power ratings. If the opening point spread is the same as that calculated using most common power ratings (e.g., Sagarin, Jim Feist), then the spread is solid and is not likely to move much prior to close. However, in those situations where there is a disparity, there is some indication that point spreads move towards those calculated by power ratings. While it is useful to use power ratings to establish the relative "class" of competing teams, they should not drive your handicapping process.

A second psychological factor that can provide you with an advantage is the way that most people make wagering decisions. They look at the point spread and then ask themselves whether it seems right. At the outset, they ascribe high validity to the point spread, thinking that line makers have a high level of omniscience. They generally feel that the line is likely to be off by only a point or two one way or the other, although as noted above, the average actual variance with respect to game outcomes is many times that.

If, after eyeballing the line, they think it is off, they then begin working through the reasons that it seems that way, essentially trying to justify their first impressions. There is a tendency to use facts selectively and to not take the time to conduct a balanced analysis. First impressions carry a lot of weight in the wagering decisions of casual bettors.

Most people are casual bettors who do not want to invest any time and energy to conduct a modicum of systematic analysis that will improve their chances of winning. This is precisely the type of person who you want to be wagering against!

As will be described in Chapter 4, the proper way to approach a game is to look at the two teams and conduct an even-handed analysis to forecast the likely point-spread difference in the outcome. To the extent that your projection varies significantly from the prevailing line, then that represents a wagering opportunity.

This takes a lot of effort if your primary objective is to search through the 100 or so games that are on the board each weekend of the regular season to find the best wagering opportunities. That is what the most serious professionals do. However, this approach is not very burdensome if you are planning to watch a game and want to place a wager to enhance your enjoyment and potentially make some money. As will be discussed in Chapter 3, you will simply adjust the amount of your wager to reflect the amount of difference between your forecasted game outcome and the point spread.

13. You must avoid psychological traps.

You can gain advantage from the wagering psychology of others. However, you need to be vigilant to ensure that you do not give back that advantage and more by falling into your own psychological traps.

The human element is a powerful force in wagering. That is why many wagering syndicates rely almost exclusively on objective computer models. These models are constructed to represent the dynamics of college basketball games but remove subjective judgment. They try to take human psychology out of the wagering equation.

Your biggest psychological risk is that you lose the right balance between wagering for entertainment and wagering to win money. It is relatively easy to have the balance tilt excessively towards entertainment, all the while claiming that it is to win money. Among the dangerous natural tendencies are:

- Wanting more action rather than less action; not being able to watch a game without having a sizeable wager on it.

- Placing bigger wagers when you have spent more time than usual handicapping a game, even if there is no clear advantage relative to the point spread

- Placing bigger wagers when watching a game with friends— to demonstrate your college basketball acumen.

- Making wagers without doing any analysis—becoming part of the dumb money.

There are also a set of psychological factors that turn objective handicapping into excessively subjective handicapping. Among the tendencies that you should watch out for are:

- Placing excessive weight on first-hand information—e.g., being highly influenced by the play of a team or a player when you watched a recent game and discounting the information from games that you didn't see.

- Placing excessive emphasis on name and reputation—just because a team has been good in the past is no guarantee that it will be good in the current season.

- Imagining things that you would like to happen for which there is no evidence. Fans consistently overestimate their favorite teams despite their actual performance in prior games.

- Bias towards favorites—it's always easier to determine the team that is likely to win and develop an argument about why it will cover than to make a compelling case for an underdog.

There are probably a dozen other psychological factors that affect wagering behavior and outcomes.

While you probably do not want to become purely a passionless investor in college basketball, you must apply some psychological discipline to avoid becoming simply another passionate fan who is only wagering for entertainment purposes.

The psychology of wagering on college basketball—both gaining benefits and mitigating risks—is addressed in later chapters. However, in general, there are three basic techniques to mitigate psychological risk.

- Adopting a standard replicable methodology for analyzing game match-ups and determining wagers so that subjective factors are properly factored into the analysis, but the typical traps are avoided.

- Adopting a mindset that it is all right to wager on almost every game, but wagers should be small unless you have a compelling analysis showing that a game is an exceptional opportunity to win. Risk is more a function of how much is wagered than how often wagers are placed.

- Keep honest records of every wager and its outcome. Maintain a running log of how well you are doing with respect to unit win rate, money won and other metrics. Try to identify biases in your wagering that create poor results and which can be corrected over the course of a season. If you find that you are cheating on yourself and keeping two sets of books, it might be wise to refrain from wagering on college basketball for awhile.

14. Comprehensive data is readily available— it is not difficult to have more data than the vast majority of people whom you are wagering against.

Before the Internet, the most critical aspect of wagering was information. Good information about players, teams or games was not readily available. A little information about an injury, a lineup change, shooting accuracy and stringency of defense went a long way in providing a wagering advantage.

It was in this environment that advisors, touts and professional gamblers flourished. They claimed to have inside information derived from their far-flung network of contacts. In fact, many touts and professional gamblers did employ and use stringers in the same way as newspapers. When the stringers came across important game information, they would phone it in and be compensated for their work. By having information that most other bettors did not have it was possible to identify teams that were undervalued by the point spreads. This was a big advantage.

Today, many bettors still believe in inside information and are intimidated by the thought that other bettors, particularly professionals, have a lot more information than they do. But that is no longer true. The information playing field has been leveled. There is very little information about college basketball teams and players that is not available on a timely basis and easily accessed by the public.

Even if you are not a professional, you can easily have access to as much information as almost anyone else placing wagers on college basketball games. It is all available via the Internet—much of it made available by the teams themselves at the official university websites. This is frequently supplemented with even more detail and analysis by additional team-specific sites created and operated by boosters and alumni. Finally, there are extremely comprehensive sites provided by ESPN, CBS, Fox and other media outlets. In fact, you can read articles about most teams in their local papers. All of this information is available to you at no cost!

Two illustrations of information that is available to the average fan illustrate how the playing field has been leveled. Early in the 2004-2005 season an important player on the University of Massachusetts basketball team was involved in an altercation and police were summoned. While some fans might have been interested in how the judicial system was going to handle the case, more were interested in the player's status for the next game. In this case, it was possible for bettors to access the campus police report and draw their own conclusions about the nature of the altercation, whether laws, school regulations or team rules were violated, and where jurisdiction for punishment, if any, might reside. Further, it was possible to go the message boards on the primary fan site for several first-hand accounts of the incident and reports on the various rumors in the athletic director and dean's offices. Anyone wagering on the next game could have all of the information available on which to make a judgment as to whether the player would be in the game.

A second example concerns "game-time decisions" regarding playing status. As in the past, whether a player is going to be held out of a game is vital information on which to make wagering decisions. When there was uncertainty about whether key players will be in the lineup it was smart to take a pass on the game. Now, in this situation, it is possible to obtain and capitalize on superior information. Using the Internet to listen to pre-game shows and the announcement of the starting lineups, you can resolve much of the uncertainty and still have time to place a bet before the game starts. Those who go to the effort to resolve such uncertainty immediately before game time are frequently rewarded with a major advantage.

These examples probably entail more effort than you will generally expend in handicapping a game and so, indeed, there will always be some bettors with more information than you. However, that number will be small and you should be comforted by the knowledge that you could have the same information if you were inclined to put in the effort. Nevertheless, the pervasiveness of information is such that the data that is readily available to you and easily accessed is more than sufficient to support the handicapping approach described in Chapter 4 and enable you to consistently win.

15. *You can attain a small advantage in wagering on the NCAA Tournament--but those games are not your best money-making opportunities.*

The NCAA Tournament always creates heightened interest in college basketball throughout the country, and at the same time an increase in formal and informal wagering. Sports books in Nevada and offshore handle large amounts of money for each game in the tournament and the weekends during which tournament games are played generate some of the biggest handles of the season.

During the NCAA tournament you not only have the entertainment value of wagering and the ability to make money, but the chance to be among the most knowledgeable about the teams and games—a chance to be treated as an expert by friends, family and co-workers. You can become the hapless soul that everyone asks: "Hey, who's going to be in the Final Four!"

Hopefully, expert status will have value to you because typically during the tournament the entertainment value goes up but the ability to win goes down!

Handicapping NCAA Tournament games to consistently win 60% of your wagers is extremely difficult and you must adjust your expectations accordingly. There are several reasons why winning is difficult. First, in contrast to the vast majority of regular season games, all tournament games are played at neutral sites. It is possible to identify strong road or home teams, but not strong neutral court teams.

Second, when possible, the NCAA Tournament committee creates interesting match-ups—ones that will be entertaining to the general public and provide opportunities for upsets. For example, there will commonly be contrasting styles—a big, slow half-court team against a small, fast, pressing team. Another common match-up is between two teams that are virtually the same in terms of playing style, strategy, and metrics (e.g., field goal percentage), yet are in different classes. One team may play in an elite conference while the opponent plays in a mid-major conference.

Third, there are an enormous number of psychological factors the effects of which cannot be easily anticipated. Some players fold under the intense pressure of a single elimination tournament, while others rise to the occasion. Some teams take lesser opponents lightly and are subject to upsets if playing teams that live to beat the big guys. Some coaches feel that their teams need a big first round margin of victory to gain confidence and momentum. Others don't care about the margin of victory. They simply want to win without burning out their starters and suffering any injuries. Some teams have incredibly loyal fans who will travel anywhere and pay anything to see their team and help make a neutral court more like a home court.

The net effect is that it is harder to forecast outcomes of NCAA Tournament games. You still will have several advantages relative to the general wagering public that will enable your unit win rate to approach 60%. The primary advantage is that you will be used to selecting a game and then handicapping it, knowing that most of the time that you will not find an enormous advantage relative to the point spread. You will be able to more quickly focus in on what is important in a match-up and figure out what factors will materially affect the game outcome. Essentially, you will be much more practiced in looking at games of the type found in the tournament and figuring out what side to bet on.

Also, you will gain an advantage if you can avoid being influenced by the media. During the tournament, point spreads are frequently influenced by the media—simply by the amount of coverage of a team in addition to what is said about it. There are examples in which the underdog darling of the media has been converted into a small favorite, but fails to cover. Therefore, you don't want to be influenced by the media, except perhaps to identify those situations in which the media hypes several underdogs and favorites relative to what the performances of those teams would indicate.

3. Principles of College Basketball Handicapping

The purpose of this chapter is to describe the key principles of handicapping college basketball games. While it is important to know what to do to analyze a game and make a wagering decision (Chapter 4), it is equally important to know *why* you are doing it. Over time, with this knowledge, you will gain some new insights and improve your college basketball handicapping techniques.

The Four Skills

Your success in wagering on college basketball depends on four skills: game analysis, data acquisition and management, money management and psychological discipline. You must be skilled in all four—a level of competence that is not difficult to achieve.

A serious deficiency in any single skill can greatly diminish your ability to consistently win. For example, if you are very good at analyzing games, but don't use that knowledge to wager rationally, then the advantage from the former is offset by the latter.

1. Analysis: Forecasting Game Outcomes

The most fundamental element of handicapping is forecasting the outcome of games more accurately than the other bettors against whom you are competing. The difference between the likely outcome of a game and that which is expected by the betting public, as represented by the point spread, is the source of wagering advantage. Knowing which team is overvalued and which is undervalued enables you to wager on the winning side of the game and to determine how much money to risk.

Game analysis is figuring out what matters and how much it matters, as embodied in two common questions:

1. "What are the indicators of game outcomes—which metrics of team performance matter and which ones don't?"
2. "To what extent is the way a team has played in the past indicative of how it is going to play in the future?"

Both of these questions are addressed in detail below and in Chapter 4.

The best forecasting is achieved through a combination of mathematics and judgment based on knowledge of college basketball. Pure mathematics allows you to simply extrapolate from past performance to future performance. Mathematical analysis is valuable and would be sufficient if games were not played and coached by humans.

However, players don't play the same way every game. Coaches recognize the strengths of their opponents and devise plans to counteract them. Teams can coalesce or fall apart very quickly. Knowledge of the game allows you to identify when and how things will change from a simple extrapolation of past performance. You have the ability to consider more qualitative factors such as changes to lineups and playing rotations, changes in style of play and strategy, injuries and suspensions, maturity and development of key players and game-specific conditions. Knowledge of the game in combination with mathematical analysis is what transforms average college basketball fans into consistently successful bettors.

2. *Information: Finding and Managing Valuable Data*

Information regarding college basketball teams and their players is pervasive. Internet access provides a wealth of detailed information to anyone with an Internet connection. Sports-information services, sports networks, newspapers and news services, and colleges themselves make information on college basketball teams readily available, and almost all of the information is free.

As described in Chapter 2, in the past bettors faced a dearth of information. Those who could get superior information had an advantage. Now, ironically, the potential problem is having too much information! Today you can get information on every play of every game and on every player on almost every Division I college basketball team. So the challenge becomes figuring out what data is important, where to get it from to ensure its quality and timeliness and how to display and manipulate it to support your analysis. It is important to recognize that data collection, storage and manipulation are simply the means to an end – supporting high quality game analysis.

Therefore, for each of the analytical techniques described in this chapter, there will be certain data that must be collected and manipulated in specific ways. The challenge will not be finding data sources; it will be to collect, store and manipulate the data efficiently. The objective in handicapping is to spend as much of your time thinking—analyzing the games—and as little of your time doing relatively menial tasks like data collection and manipulation. Therefore, data collection and management is as much about saving time as supporting analysis.

3. *Money Management*

"Money management" is about deploying your bankroll in a way that balances your desire to consistently win a lot of money with the risk of losing all of your money. You must ensure that the entertainment of wagering on college basketball doesn't overwhelm good financial management and discipline. Money management does not entail sophisticated accounting or financial systems – it is simply the disciplined application of a few basic principles regarding when to wager and how much to risk.

The most fundamental principle of money management is to risk your money on the best wagering opportunities and not risk much money on games in which you have no advantage—ones in which you are wagering primarily for entertainment. This translates to a very simple rule: The amount that you wager on a game should be related to the certainty of winning. You should wager more on "sure things" than on games in which the point spread seems accurate. Don't delude yourself about which are which!

A professional college basketball investor will spend a lot of time to find games in which there is a big advantage—where the line seems to be wrong. He is not concerned about what teams are involved or whether the game is televised. He is simply looking for good investments and will only put money at risk when he thinks he finds one. Even professional college basketball investors will apply the simple rule and calibrate the amounts they wager based on how big an advantage they think they have found.

The strategy of a professional college basketball investor is like that of a professional blackjack player. College basketball investors may evaluate dozens of games to find a good investment opportunity, and when they find one, place a big bet. Professional blackjack players will play dozens of hands for low stakes waiting for a favorable deck. When a deck turns in their favor, they place large wagers to try to capitalize on their advantage. The size of their wagers directly corresponds to how favorable a deck becomes for the players.

Your situation is likely to be different. You will be interested in a specific game and will enjoy watching or listening to it. However, you would like to enhance your enjoyment and make some money by wagering on it. Sometimes a game of personal interest will provide a great wagering opportunity; most of the time it will not. Therefore, you must analyze the game and then place a wager that is consistent with your advantage relative to the point spread, if any. Most of the time you will be making modest bets, but there will be times when large wagers are justified. It is critical that you separate the entertainment value of a game from the investment value of a game when you determine the amount of money you risk.

Keep in mind that pure investors in college basketball find that only about 10% of the games offer an excellent wagering opportunity—that is, the point spread is way off from the likely outcome of the game. That is also likely to be true for you during the course of the season. It is easier to attain a 60% unit rate and generate large winnings if you vary your wagers appropriately by carefully selecting games on which to bet.

Consider the following example. Suppose the wagering opportunities fall into three categories—excellent, good and fair-- each of which occurs with a different frequency and has a different win rate. The 10% of the wagering opportunities that are considered excellent justify a 10-unit wager, while the 50% of fair opportunities justify only a three-unit wager. In wagering on 40 games the outcomes might be as follows:

	Pct./No. of Opportunities	Win Rate	Wagered (Units) Avg	Total	Results (Units) Won	Lost
Excellent	10%/4	75%	10	40	30.0	10.0
Good	40%/16	60%	7	112	67.2	44.8
Fair	50%/20	50%	3	60	30.0.	30.0
				212	127.2	84.8
Average					60%	40%

If everything remains the same and the amounts wagered are not varied—assume that five units are wagered on each game—then the unit win rate is reduced from 60% to only 56%. Over the course of a full season that makes a huge difference in your winnings and the return on your bankroll.

	Pct./No. of Opportunities	Win Rate	Wagered (Units) Avg.	Wagered (Units) Total	Results(Units) Won	Results(Units) Lost
Excellent	10%/4	75%	5	20	15	5
Good	40%/16	60%	5	80	48	32
Fair	50%/20	50%	5	100	50	50
				200	113	87
Average					56%	44%

The greatest upside is generated by identifying those games in which there is a significant advantage relative to the point spread and placing larger wagers.

4. Discipline

The greatest threat to winning is a lack of discipline. For those who are simply wagering for entertainment purposes and are not too concerned about winning, this is not a problem. The number and size of wagers simply corresponds to how much enjoyment will be realized from the action itself.

For those who are pure investors in college basketball—interested in winning money and not too concerned about entertainment—the nature of disciplined investing is quite clear. If an objective analysis doesn't show a compelling opportunity to win, then a wager should not be placed on a game.

However, when a person is wagering for both entertainment and to win—and is willing to make tradeoffs between the two—it is more difficult to define precisely the discipline that is required. The more one seeks entertainment, the more one is likely to sacrifice winnings, and those preferences can change from day to day and from game to game.

How and when you make these tradeoffs is a personal matter, as long as you realize you are making them. A key element of wagering discipline is to prevent self-delusion—that is, ensure that when you place a wager with the objective of winning that the decision is not made and amount placed at risk based on irrational logic driven by an excessive desire for action.

There are three examples of poor logic that are common threats to wagering discipline.

- ***Due to win.*** Some betters think that after a series of losses that they are "due to win" and that at that time they should increase the amounts that they wager so as to quickly recoup their losses. However, there is no such thing as being due to win. Each wager is independent. The outcome of today's wager does not have anything to do with yesterday's wager any more than today's game between, say, Purdue and Iowa has anything to do with yesterday's game between Duke and North Carolina. Ironically, those people that subscribe to the "due to win" theory don't seem to subscribe to a "due to lose" theory. They prefer the "I'm on a hot streak" theory. It simply reveals human nature: Most people would like to find a reason to wager on more games or place greater amounts of money at risk.

- ***First-hand experience.*** People tend to place much more value and weight on information derived from a first-hand experience than secondary sources. Watching or listening to games creates very strong impressions about the teams and players participating that will influence future wagering decisions. Watching a team play extremely well creates a subconscious bias towards a team. It is critical to be alert to this effect since there are likely to be certain teams that you will watch or listen to frequently, and as a result you may develop strong biases. That is not to say that it is unwise to watch teams play. It can provide some real insight to be used to your advantage in the future. But it is important to guard against excessive bias to put what you see first hand in the context of what you see second hand.

- *Names and reputations.* If you are a basketball fan, you probably have opinions and perceptions about many teams. The risk is that those perceptions and opinions are developed over many seasons and may not reflect the capabilities of teams during the current season. Teams change from year to year, even those in excellent programs. For example, teams like North Carolina, Kansas and Duke are presumed to be very good every year—until proven otherwise. North Carolina won 30 games during the 2000-2001 season, then hit bottom with a 9-21 record the following year, and only four years later won the national championship. Conversely, each new entry to Division I is assumed to be bad until it shows that it isn't. There is a tendency to discount the ability and chances of schools that you have never heard of. Today, there is more parity among the top 150 Division I teams than ever before, and it is more common that the relative performance of a team substantially improves or deteriorates from season to season. It is important to stay current and to discount names and reputations when handicapping games.

Game Analysis and Wagering Decisions

There are 13 basic principles in analyzing college basketball games and making wagering decisions. Understanding and applying these principles intelligently enables you to significantly increase your win rate. They provide the underlying logic for the step-by-step process of analyzing games and making wagering decisions described in Chapter 4. While these principles are highly focused on wagering on point-spread propositions, they are generally applicable to other common types of college basketball propositions.

1. The basis for your wager is the difference between what you forecast the outcome of a game to be and the point spread— large differences are better than small differences!

The point spread for a game represents the consensus of the betting public regarding the game's outcome. While line makers create an opening line, the wagering public determines the final point spread by voting with its wagered dollars. However, the consensus opinion of the wagering public is not necessarily an excellent indicator of outcomes. As noted earlier, the average differences between actual game outcomes and final point spreads ranges from seven to 10 points, depending on the conference. That is a wide variance and offers considerable opportunity to handicappers with the ability to forecast outcomes more accurately than the general wagering public.

That is what you are trying to do—forecast the outcome of games more accurately than the wagering public. By putting in a little more time than the average bettor, using better forecasting techniques than the average better and using more data than the average bettor, you can achieve that goal relatively easily.

As emphasized earlier, the amounts that you will wager should be scaled to how great the difference is between what you think the outcome of the game is going to be and the perceptions of the wagering public. Therefore, it is necessary to give more attention to figuring out how big the difference is than finding that there is one. Remember: The point spread is much more accurate with respect to forecasting the team that will win than it is in forecasting the margin of victory.

2. *Your biggest advantage is gained when you can identify when a team's performance in the next game will be different than it has been in most of its previous games.*

All but the most casual bettors use the past to predict the future. Game logs showing how a team has played in prior games are pervasive. Most logs provide basic information on game dates, locations, scores, and performance against the spread. Any bettor who does any analysis whatsoever will consult a game log to see how a team has done in the past, to draw some conclusions about how the team is playing, and then, by extension, to assess how the team is likely to perform that night.

There is some merit to this approach since in forecasting individual or team performance there is a good likelihood that the performance in the next game will be similar to that of the prior games. In fact, this is true in just about all types of economic, financial and behavioral forecasting as well. You should respect past performance but fully recognize that all elements of past performance are not equally useful in forecasting future performance. You must be selective in what you look at and treat as relevant.

The biggest advantage gained by the best college basketball handicappers, as well as economic and financial forecasters, is identifying when the immediate future will be different than the past—anticipating change. Doing so is difficult. But you can be reasonably sure that when you do it, the wagering public will not have done it and that there will be a big difference between the point spread and the expected outcome of the game.

Coaches seek consistency and steady improvement from their team during the season. However, that is rarely achieved. The performance of a team in any game is affected by dozens of factors, any one of which can suddenly become of paramount importance. Also, teams are made up of players. The development and the chemistry among players can take a team in many directions, as evidenced by the fact that some teams actually get worse as the season progresses.

Nevertheless, there are some reliable indicators regarding when team performance is changing or change is imminent. In some measure, this is an advantage that can be gained by college basketball fans that are looking at a team's past performance with some insight regarding how coaches coach and players play. Pure mathematical models are excellent at forecasting future performance by extrapolating from past performance, but are not very reliable at anticipating *changes* in performance. The combination of rudimentary mathematics and knowledge of the sport will be most effective in anticipating change.

3. *Very recent trends are the best predictors of change in performance.*

As in any type of forecasting, it is difficult to tell when a team's performance in the next game is going to be different than the other games played during the season. However, the performance of college basketball teams can change with some frequency, so going to the effort of anticipating change is worthwhile. There are two ways to forecast change: by identifying recent team performance trends and by anticipating the effect of game-specific circumstances.

The best way to identify when changes in performance are likely to occur is by looking at trends from recent games. The key question is: What is the evidence of a reliable trend that is material to your wagering decision?

There are three considerations: duration, frequency and cause. You only need to look at the most recent games in a commonsense way, rather than using sophisticated mathematical models.

First, in identifying a trend you should only look at games during the previous five or six weeks—approximately 10 games. It is very unusual that anything that happens in games prior to that time is part of a trend, and if it is, it is well known and factored in by much of the wagering public. The 10 games provide a baseline perspective on a team's play and help identify broad trends. However, the meaningful trends that are less obvious to the wagering public are more likely to occur during the previous three or four games.

Second, there should be statistical evidence that something has changed. The results and many of the measurable statistics from very recent games should look different from earlier games—not simply in one game, but three or four games. Don't attach too much significance to one game, particularly the immediately preceding game. Teams have great games and poor games, but there is little likelihood of duplicating those extreme feats in the next game.

Third, there is a temptation to simply look at numbers. Three or four consecutive convincing covers is a trend. Hitting 50% of all shots from the field in three or four consecutive games against decent competition is a trend. However, you should ask yourself why those things have occurred. What has changed in the play of the team? This is the best means of satisfying yourself that you have identified a true trend and not simply a statistical anomaly. Determining the "why" may be more difficult than identifying the "what."

Among the common causes of changed performance that you might want to check for are:

- Starting lineup and rotation
- Shot selection—e.g., mix of two- and three-point field goal attempts
- Defense strategy—e.g., playing a zone
- Maturation of a point guard—e.g., turnovers, assists, points
- Lesser competition
- Home games

These examples illustrate two types of situations that dictate different actions. The first four examples are causes of change related to the way the team plays. They are within the team's control and can plausibly be perpetuated in future games. The latter two examples may also explain the recent trend, but are not within the team's control. If the team's next opponent and venue are quite different, the most recent trend may not be as relevant in forecasting performance.

The second means of predicting change is to anticipate the effect of impending events. This means is less common and less reliable. A common example is the first home game after a string of road games. A similar example is Senior Night for a team that has been successful and has a lot of senior starters. A third example is the return to the lineup of a star player after a long layoff. The first two examples typically result in better team play relative to the point spread. The third example results in worse play relative to the point spread since the return of such players frequently does not have the potent effect on a game's outcome that may be widely anticipated.

4. Don't waste time handicapping games than can't be handicapped.

The games that you don't wager on are as valuable as those on which you do.

There are certain types of games for which it is particularly difficult to forecast outcomes and determine whether there is an advantage relative to the point spread. While you are wagering for entertainment as well as to win money, neither is fully achieved when the outcomes of games are highly unpredictable and your chances of winning are no better than 50%.

The general rule is to avoid a game when things occur that will affect the outcome in unpredictable ways. The most common occurrences of this type are when important players miss games or rejoin the team, the teams are playing in very strange locations or at a very unusual time (e.g., tournaments, when games could start early in the morning or late at night), and very early season games before there is really any past performance to analyze.

There is simply no way to predict the effect of changes in key personnel. It is difficult to forecast how a team will play without a key player. Sometimes the rest of the team steps up and plays at unexpectedly high levels, especially for a game or two. At other times, teams are disorganized and lack rhythm. Similarly, there is the situation in which a key player who has been out rejoins the team. There is a natural tendency to expect that the team will be much improved relative to its performance without him. That is not necessarily the case. Sometimes the returning player is out of shape and unpracticed and cannot play at his normal skill level. Sometimes, the return of a player disrupts what has become a sound playing rotation. At other times, the player lifts the team well above the level of play before his return.

The most common type of game that you should avoid is a "mismatch". When one team is presumed to be more than 12 points better than another, the two teams are not really in the same class. When the better team is at home the point spread will be 15 or 16; on the road it will be 8 or 9. There is little doubt about which team will win. However, there is inherently high variability in the margin of victory in such games. The variability comes from player psychology and coaching decisions more than the inherent skills of the teams.

You can be sure that a coach wants to win every game that his team plays. However, once the winner is determined, margin of victory is not very important to most coaches. They frequently use the opportunity of a large victory margin to achieve other coaching objectives. They rarely try to maximize margin of victory.

Yet for this reason, when a point spread is very low you can have more confidence in forecasting a game's outcome. If the line is one point, there is no question that both coaches will be trying to win throughout the game. In this situation a coach who is trying to win is, implicitly, also trying to cover the point spread. While the favorite may win by 10 points, the margin of victory is immaterial to your wager. The bigger the point spread, the less either coach is going to share your personal objective of covering the spread

Where do coaching decisions come into play in a mismatch? The coach of the better team that can win comfortably may desire to rest players for the next game, get his bench players more time on the court to build experience and depth, or even show some sportsmanship by not embarrassing the other team. At other times, the same coach may feel that his team must annihilate its opponent to build its confidence and to gain momentum for the next game.

Similarly, some coaches of lesser teams will try to make a bad loss look close by continuing to play starters after the game is out of reach to pick up as many garbage points as possible at the end of the game. At other times, the same coach will use it as an opportunity to get everyone into the game and reward bench players for their dedication during the season.

The only exception to the general rule of avoiding mismatches is if a team demonstrates near perfect consistency in mismatch games— they always cover because the coach and team find it exhilarating to beat lesser teams or they never cover because the coach and team believe that running up the score is unsportsmanlike.

The track record of the top 16 seeds in the 2005 NCAA Tournament illustrates the lack of consistency in mismatch games by top teams. During the regular season, these teams played many games in which the spread was at least 10 points, but with one exception, there was no significant pattern to outcomes relative to the spread.

The one exception was Duke. As a heavy favorite—more than 20 points—Duke covered the spread in all five of its games. When the point spread was only 10-20 points, Duke failed to cover eight of nine times. This may be sufficient evidence of Duke's playing tendencies to justify a wager in a mismatch game involving Duke, but this is a strange pattern of outcomes that does not inspire wagering confidence.

A common question is: Why not look at the records of the lesser teams in a mismatch to see if there is any pattern? In a mismatch, the lesser team has very little influence on the outcome. Also, less skilled teams perform less consistently. Even if there is the will to rise to the occasion against better teams, there may not be the ability to do so on a consistent basis.

There is one final situation in which wagering should be avoided: asymmetrical information. That is the situation in which you have a lot of information about one team but very little about the other. It is hard to compare one team to another when there is not roughly the same information available. This situation does not occur very frequently for teams in Division I. It is most likely to occur very early in the season or in postseason tournaments when there is wagering on some teams that typically are not on the board.

		Against the Spread	
Seed	Team	Spread 10-20	Spread >20
1	Duke	1-8	5-0
1	North Carolina	8-2	5-3
1	Illinois	6-4-1	1-2
1	Washington	6-2	0
2	Connecticut	4-3	1-0
2	Oklahoma St.	4-5-1	2-0
2	Wake Forest	5-2	0-2-1
2	Kentucky	4-2	2-2-1
3	Kansas	6-9	0
3	Arizona	6-5	0-2
3	Gonzaga	4-5	0-3
3	Oklahoma	3-4	1-0
4	Louisville	4-2	6-3
4	Florida	4-4	1-1
4	Syracuse	4-5	1-2
4	Boston College	0-2-1	0-1

5. *Beware of season-to-date averages.*

It is now possible to easily obtain cumulative averages for all metrics of team performance--outcome, scoring, field goal shooting, defense, rebounding, turnovers, assists and free throw percentage. A common mistake of many college basketball handicappers is to assume that season-to-date or cumulative averages are very meaningful.

These statistics always would be useful if the next opponent is truly the average of all prior opponents, but it is not. The next opponent is defined by its overall team strength (i.e., class), its typical style of play and playing tendencies at home and on the road. Therefore, it is the averages for games against *like* opponents under similar circumstances that are valuable, not the cumulative averages against all opponents.

For example, many teams have pre-conference schedules that are substantially weaker or stronger than their conference schedules. Consider all of the major teams that have cupcakes on their early season schedule— the games are such mismatches and so unpredictable that sports books do not set lines and accept wagers. A team can roll up some impressive victories and impressive statistics against weak competition. However, when it is time to play stronger teams of comparable strength, the same outcomes should not be expected.

Consider Georgetown's performance in the 2003-2004 season. Georgetown won its first 10 games against lesser teams—Grambling, Penn State, Coastal Carolina, Delaware State, Norfolk State, Davidson, Elon, Howard, Citadel and Rutgers. It won by an average of 19 points and its cumulative statistics appeared very impressive. Georgetown was 2-3 against the spread for the five games that were on the board—five games were off the board.

In early January, when Georgetown faced real opponents, the story was quite different. It went 1-5 straight up and 0-6 against the spread, failing to cover by an average of 6.7 points.

Date	Site	Opponent	Score	SU	ATS
1/6/04	H	Boston College	64-72	L	L
1/10/04	A	West Virginia	58-62	L	L
1/14/04	A	Connecticut	70-94	L	L
1/20/04	H	St. Johns	71-69	W	L
1/24/04	H	Duke	66-85	L	L
1/26/04	A	Providence	50-65	L	L

Georgetown continued to spiral downward. After its 10-0 start Georgetown went 3-15 straight up and 3-15 against the spread for the remainder of the season. The statistics from the final 18 games were ugly. It was a little surprising that Georgetown continued to get worse faster than the market could adjust and that it failed to cover its last seven games. However, it was not too surprising that at the end of the season Georgetown replaced its coach.

A second example concerns the top 16 seeds in the 2005 NCAA tournament. Each team made it to the second round, where the competition was stiff. Looking at those teams, a high percentage of their games were played against lesser competition in which they were favored by more than 10 points or the game wasn't even on the board. None of those games would be useful in forecasting performance in second round Tournament games. Essentially, between 30% and 75% of all games played by each team and their associated statistical performance were virtually irrelevant in forecasting the outcome of their second round game.

#1 Seeds	Duke (14), North Carolina (19), Illinois (21), Washington (9)
#2 Seeds	Connecticut (8), Oklahoma St. (16), Wake Forest (12), Kentucky (14)
#3 Seeds	Kansas (16), Arizona (13), Gonzaga (13), Oklahoma (11)
#4 Seeds	Louisville (18), Florida (13), Syracuse (15), Boston College (9)

Therefore, apples-to-apples comparisons are critical. It is valuable to distinguish the performance in comparable games from averages for a team's entire schedule. It is frequently quite amazing how different the averages turn out to be. This principle is addressed in more depth in Subsection 7.

6. Revealing a team's true performance against the point spread provides the best indicator of a trend.

The most pervasive statistics on websites focused on college basketball wagering are related to the performance of a team against the point spread (ATS).

You should look at these statistics, but perhaps not in the way that the sports wagering industry typically displays them. ATS is the indicator of how a team actually performs relative to the consensus of the betting public. If it consistently fails to cover, it has underperformed and is a worse team than the wagering public expected. If it consistently covers, it has over-performed and is a better team than the wagering public expected.

College basketball wagering is a market that adjusts to a team's performance. If a team fails to cover five consecutive games, the wagering public will see the underperformance trend. The wagering public will be less inclined to wager on that team. In future games, the point spread will move towards that team in order to induce people to bet on it. Over time the market adjusts and the teams will begin to cover again.

ATS is only a gross indicator of how well a team's actual performance compares to that expected by the wagering public and can only be used to identify broad trends. Because the market adjusts and tends to prevent long streaks, simply looking at wins and losses against the point spread is most frequently inconclusive and reveals no actionable trend. Over a 10 game span, most teams will be 5-5, 6-4 or 4-6.

The more important indicators are the average number of points by which a team covers when it covers and the average number of point by which a team fails to cover when it doesn't cover.

A team that is 5-5 ATS, but fails to cover by an average of two points will offer much more value than one that fails to cover by an average of 10 points. A team for which the average cover margin is 10 points is a more comfortable wager than one for which the average cover margin is two points.

Similarly, a team that usually covers and covers by an increasing margin over time is a team that is getting better and stronger—and it is doing so faster than the market can recognize it and adjust accordingly. This is usually a sign of a very promising wagering opportunity.

As an example, look at the midseason performance of Dayton during the 2003-2004 season. During an eight-game span of creditable conference competition, Dayton went 8-0 straight up and 7-1 ATS. It appeared to be a very strong team. However, while Dayton was indeed a strong team that ultimately received an NCAA berth, it was not as strong as the simple ATS statistics made it appear.

Opponent	Closing Spread	Game Outcome	Cover Margin
Temple	-3.5	-4.0	-0.5
At Richmond	-4.5	-5.0	-0.5
At Fordham	-9.5	-19.0	-9.5
George Washington	-5.5	-8.0	-2.5
At La Salle	-4.5	-2.0	+2.5
Xavier	-3.0	-7.0	-4.0
Richmond	-3.5	-5.0	-1.5
At Massachusetts	-14.0	-14.5	-0.5

While Dayton consistently covered, it was by the narrowest of margins. Excluding the game against Fordham, the worst team in the conference that season, the average cover was by only 1.5 points. While Dayton got credit for performing up to the expectations of the wagering pubic, it could not be concluded that Dayton dominated against the point spread, or that it is was an improving college basketball juggernaut.

Duquesne offers a second example during the same season. As a weak team in the Atlantic 10, a light pre-conference schedule had been carefully crafted to gain some early wins. Duquesne's home games were against Prairie View, Siena, Pitt, Loyola (Md.) George Mason, Robert Morris and Cornell. As expected, Duquesne won four and lost three, but it was 0-5 ATS (the Prairie View and Robert Morris games were not on the board). Not only did it consistently fail to cover, the average margin was 7.4 points. Shown below is the entire game log prior to the game at Rhode Island in early January.

Site	Opponent	Closing Spread	Game Outcome	Cover Margin
H	Prairie View	NL	-20	---
H	Siena	-1.0	+10	+11
H	Pittsburgh	-13.5	-14	+.5
H	Loyola (Md)	-18.5	-9	+9.5
A	W. Virginia	+12.5	+4	-8.5
A	Akron	+10	+3	-7
H	George Mason	+2.5	+10	+7.5
A	Minnesota	+14.5	+5	-9.5
H	Robert Morris	NL	-21	---
H	Cornell	-9.5	-1	+8.5
A	Richmond	+14.5	+3	-11.5

With a dubious home court performance, road expectations were modest throughout the early season. Certainly, the two impressive covers at West Virginia and Akron could not have been anticipated. By the third road game at Minnesota, some handicappers could have had an inkling that Duquesne would cover by 9.5 points. However, by the fourth road game at Richmond, those tracking cover margins would certainly have revealed strong road performance—beyond simply covering the spread. Finally, by the fifth road game at Rhode Island, there was still a major wagering opportunity. Duquesne covered by 27.5 points!

Looking at results ATS and cover margins for road games was the means of identifying a very powerful trend which could be transformed to very profitable wagering opportunities. Shown below are the entries for the game log that make the trend obvious.

Opponent	Closing Spread	Game Outcome	Cover Margin
At West Virginia	12.5	4.0	-8.5
At Akron	10.0	3.0	-7.5
At Minnesota	14.5	5.0	-9.5
At Richmond	14.5	3.0	-11.5
At Rhode Island	10.5	-17.0	-27.5

A team's performance against the point spread—cover margin as well as wins and losses—is a very powerful indicator of playing performance. It shows how the team plays relative to the expectations of the wagering public, and it can isolate trends that are not very obvious to most bettors who will be competing with you. Part of the power of cover margins is that it is a statistic that is not readily provided by the dozens of wagering-related websites. Consequently, it is not frequently used. However, while cover margins are not readily provided, they can be computed in just a few minutes from commonly available game logs that display closing point spreads and final scores.

7. There are meaningful differences in home and road performance.

Home court advantage is a well-documented aspect of college basketball. Teams do better at home because they are playing on a familiar court with a supportive crowd. Also, in some measure, teams are thought to play better at home because the players believe they will play better at home.

Conversely, a team's caliber of play on the road might be diminished by many factors. Travel fatigue can cause problems, particularly when playing Thursday and Saturday road games in different locations or encountering bad weather that can convert a one-hour chartered flight into a six-hour bus ride. There are also potential environmental distractions. Winter road trips to Hawaii create legendary lapses in performance. Finally, hostile crowds can be really hostile!

The combination of these factors creates a home court advantage. The real issue is how material is it in terms of playing performance and outcomes. How does a team play at home, and is it substantially different than how it plays on the road? As illustrated above for Duquesne, the differences can be extraordinary, although not typically in the manner demonstrated by Duquesne.

Playing venue will be worth considering in more than 90% of the games you handicap. While there are games played on neutral courts early in the season, neutral-court games after January 1 are rare.

The conventional wisdom is that the home team has a four point advantage. In reality, the advantage probably ranges from two points to as many as five points. The low end of the range tends to occur when a team plays in a big multiuse arena in its home town. The arena is not really home, it may be rarely filled with fans, and the fans may be too distant from the court to affect the opponent. Two examples are St. Johns (Madison Square Garden) and Georgetown (MCI Center).

At the other extreme, regardless of the level, is Duke playing at Cameron Indoor Stadium, New Mexico playing in "The Pit" and Penn playing at the Palestra against non-Philadelphia teams. In addition to familiar surroundings, fan support is extraordinary.

A factor that affects home court advantage is the relative experience of the two teams. Teams that are loaded with seniors, many of whom have played 40-50 road games by their senior year, are less susceptible to road conditions. In contrast, teams with a lot of freshmen and junior college transfers have problems on the road and, in fact, may not be particularly adept at defending their home court either. Very early in the season there are wagering opportunities found when a very talented team with lots of freshmen plays a team with lesser talent but four or five senior starters. The latter team is a good wagering opportunity. When the two teams play toward the end of the season, the younger team is probably the one to take. It must be recognized that players mature during the season and the effect of playing on the road diminishes. Nevertheless, such a tendency cannot be assumed; it must be validated

There is a caution about assessing home court advantage. Most of the better teams in Division I have scheduling leverage; they can arrange to have more than half of their games at home. Also, they can schedule lesser teams prior to the conference season. The home court advantage may be inflated by playing less competitive teams at home than on the road.

In summary, this is another case in which making the right comparison is important. In evaluating a match-up, it is usually desirable to compare the home team's home performance and the road team's road performance.

8. *Past performance against teams comparable to the next opponent provides a very good indicator of how a team will play.*

The best indicator of how a team will play in an upcoming game is how it has played against similar teams under similar circumstances. The performance metrics (e.g., field goal percentages, rebounds, assists, turnovers) for these games are the most relevant for forecasting future games. Isolating comparable games and the associated statistics is a key to a reliable match-up analysis.

Each team has a talent level and a style of play designed to best take advantage of its talent. Each team will play better against some styles than others, and its performance statistics show it. It is a mistake to think that all teams are largely the same and that the results of one game are as good a predictor of future performance as another.

Three attributes are most relevant in identifying comparable opponents.

- *Class.* The most important games in a team's record are those against teams in the same class as the current opponent— roughly the same strength and talent level. Comparability can be established by looking at various well-respected power ratings, such as Sagarin. For example, if the current opponent has a power rating of 85, then comparable opponents are teams played with ratings from approximately 80 to 90. The way a team plays against opponents with ratings 95 or 75— those that are much better or much worse—are not relevant when the immediate opponent is not in those classes. Also, as the difference in class increases, the likelihood of a game being a mismatch increases and it is unwise to wager any significant amounts of money on such games.

  While most power ratings do not reliably predict the final margin of victory, they are sufficiently accurate to indicate the relative class of two teams.

- *Style.* Each team has a preferred playing strategy and tries to capitalize on its talent. Some teams are very athletic, but may have few highly skilled players, and therefore like to run the court and wear down their opponents. Some teams are highly skilled, but not very athletic and try to win with solid defense and a machine-like half-court offense. There are three or four other common playing styles. In looking at a match-up, you should look at how well a team has done against teams that play the same style as its immediate opponent—does its style prevail, or does the other team force a change in approach?

  Figuring out opponents' styles from commonly available information sources—team logs and box scores—is not always easy. As a practical matter, you should simply seek to identify the extremes as well as possible from data that is readily available—very high or low scoring teams, teams that rely on shooting (and making) lots of three pointers, or teams that apply pressure throughout the game seeking turnovers and wearing out the opponents.

71

- *Time.* Recent games are the most relevant; November games are irrelevant in February. Therefore, in identifying comparable games played, only those played in the preceding five or six weeks can be considered relevant.

As an example, consider the log for George Washington during the 2004-2005 season immediately prior to its March 1 home game against St. Joseph's (Figure 3-1). Games prior to January 12 are not relevant and should be ignored. St. Joseph's had a power rating of 88. Of the 12 games played since January 12, those involving teams with power rating between 83 and 93 are comparable—Xavier (twice), Temple, Richmond and Dayton (twice).

Of these four teams, none plays exactly like St. Joseph's. St. Joseph is an experienced team that, while not physically gifted, plays very tough defense and has a highly disciplined half-court offense with lots of screens to create shots for its three point shooters. Dayton is the most similar in style, but is young and inexperienced. Temple plays very tough defense, but is physical and not very organized on offense. However, together the six games and four opponents constitute a meaningful set of comparables.

Therefore, the comparison of real value is to be made between George Washington's performance statistics in these six games relative to St. Joseph's performance statistics against teams comparable to George Washington.

9. *Isolate the handful of metrics of team performance that most affect the outcome of games.*

There are dozens of metrics of every college basketball team's performance that are made publicly available by sports media and the schools themselves. Offensive and defensive statistics are available for most teams and their players on a game-by-game and cumulative basis.

Greater use of statistics is a trend in all sports. It is easy to collect and make statistics available to the public. Also, many websites and

Figure 3-1: George Washington University Log

Date	Site	Opponent	Rating	Outcome	Line	S/U	ATS
3/18/2005	N	GEORGIA TECH	97.5	68-80	6	L	L
3/12/2005	N	ST. JOSEPH'S	90.5	76-67	-2.5	W	W
3/11/2005	N	TEMPLE	87	77-58	-2.5	W	W
3/10/2005	N	FORDHAM	82	79-63	-11.5	W	W
3/5/2005	A	RHODE ISLAND	78	68-39	-7	W	W
3/1/2005	H	ST. JOSEPH'S	88.5	56-71	-7	L	L
2/26/2005	A	DAYTON	86	62-59	-2	W	W
2/23/2005	A	XAVIER	85.5	62-81	-2.5	L	L
2/19/2005	H	DUQUESNE	75	80-57	-20	W	W
2/16/2005	H	FORDHAM	82	80-70	-17	W	L
2/12/2005	H	RICHMOND	81.5	80-63	-12.5	W	W
2/5/2005	A	TEMPLE	92.5	74-58	3.5	W	W

Figure 3-1: George Washington University Log (cont.)

Date	Site	Opponent		Score			
1/30/2005	H	DAYTON	84	82-73	-11	W	L
1/25/2005	H	XAVIER	85.5	65-66	-9.5	L	L
1/22/2005	A	RICHMOND	83	59-70	-4	L	L
1/19/2005	A	LA SALLE	76	84-66	-12.5	W	W
1/15/2005	H	MASSACHUSETTS	79.5	74-76*	-17	L	L
1/12/2005	A	ST. BONAVENTURE	71	85-59	-20.5	W	W
1/8/2005	A	DUQUESNE	75	81-57	-10	W	W
1/5/2005	H	LA SALLE	79	71-42	-17	W	W
12/29/2004	A	WEST VIRGINIA	92	65-71	3.5	L	L
12/23/2004	A	FLORIDA INT'L	73	81-71	-13	W	L
12/18/2004	H	TOWSON STATE	73	85-69	-26	W	L
12/11/2004	A	ST. FRANCIS (PA)	75	79-65		W	
12/5/2004	N	MARYLAND	102.5	101-92	6	W	W
12/4/2004	H	MICHIGAN STATE	98.5	96-83	6.5	W	W
12/1/2004	H	MOUNT ST. MARY'S	68.5	81-58		W	
11/28/2004	H	FAIRFIELD	81	87-70	-12.5	W	W
11/20/2004	H	MORGAN STATE	65	94-70		W	
11/15/2004	A	WAKE FOREST	97.5	76-97	13	L	L

media sources want to attract users by having the most comprehensive content and statistics. The statistics available to the public reflects the way that coaching staffs now use data. Among the major college basketball programs in the country, the performance of each player and entire teams are quantified in excruciating detail. For example, some programs keep track of such things as the average number of passes or touches before two-point and three-point field goal attempts!

The key question for the college basketball handicapper is: What statistics should I pay attention to? The more fundamental question is: What performance metrics are the best predictors of game outcomes?

Professional college basketball handicappers will answer: It depends on the teams that are playing. That is not very helpful to someone who is not making wagering on college basketball his life's work. In fact, there are only five sets of metrics for team performance that largely explain game outcomes. By efficiently looking at those metrics, you can develop a pretty good idea of what is likely to happen in a game.

- Field goal shooting (offensive and defensive)
- Ball handling (turnovers and assists)
- Rebounding
- Free throws
- Team depth

Before identifying the specific performance metrics, there are two cautions. First, in many cases, you must look at a team's performance metrics relative to those of the opponent. A team's three-point field goal percentage is interesting, but most meaningful when compared to the opponent's three-point field goal defensive percentage. Similarly, a team's turnover frequency is particularly relevant when compared to the opponent's tendency to create turnovers.

Second, there is some interdependence among performance metrics. That is, if some metrics are very positive, others are also likely to be positive because they are caused by the same thing. For example, teams that get a high percentage of their scoring by the frontcourt typically also have strong rebounding metrics—particularly offensive rebounds. Offensive rebounds are frequently converted to field goals as high percentage shots.

Unless you recognize this effect, you will almost always decide that you should wager on the favorite. Favorites usually will look better on many performance metrics, and to the extent that some metrics are positively related, those teams probably look better than they actually are. Consider the example above. If the opponent is successful in hitting the boards and rebounding well, it diminishes both the team's rebounding margin and frontcourt scoring.

In looking at performance metrics, the favorite almost always looks like the better team. That's why it is the favorite. However, it is generally not the better team by as much as the numbers might lead you to believe. The important thing is being able to put the numbers in perspective, and using your knowledge of the game, see when and how underdogs will do better than indicated by their numbers.

Each of the five key performance metrics are described below and summarized in Figure 3-2.

Figure 3-2
Primary Metrics of Team Performance

Field Goals Shooting

- Two-point field goal shooting percentage—offense
- Two-point field goal shooting percentage—defense
- Three-point field goal shooting percentage—offense
- Three-point field goal shooting percentage—defense
- Percentage of three-point shots—offense
- Percentage of three-point shots—defense

Ball-handling

- Average turnovers
- Average turnover margin
- Average assists
- Average assists margin
- Assists-to-turnovers ratio (ATO)

Rebounding

- Average rebounding margin

Free Throws

- Average free throw attempt margin

Team Depth

- Players averaging >10 minutes per game

Field Goal Shooting (Offensive and Defensive)

Teams that shoot well are more desirable than those that shoot poorly. The seemingly obvious thing to do would be to give a lot of weight to a team's field goal shooting percentage. However, overall field goal percentage– can be misleading.

Field goal percentage depends on two things—shooting skill and shot selection. Three-point field goals are harder to make than two-point field goals. Three-point field goal percentages are lower than two point field goal percentages. The greater the percentage of shots that are taken from behind the arc, the lower the team's overall field goal percentage.

Consider the example below for two teams. Both take the same number of shots and are equally skilled in shooting two- and three-pointers. However, Team 1 has a much better overall field goal percentage. But it only results in a two point scoring advantage

Team 1

	Taken	Made	Pct. Made	Points
Two Point Shots	50	25	50%	50
Three Point Shots	10	3	30%	9
Total	60	28	47%	59

Team 2

	Taken	Made	Pct. Made	Points
Two Point Shots	30	15	50%	30
Three Point Shots	30	9	30%	27
Total	60	24	40%	57

Therefore, the three most useful metrics for field goals shooting are two-point field goal percentage, three-point field goal percentage and the percentage of three-point shots relative to all shots taken.

Almost as important as how a team shoots is its ability to defend the shot. Preventing the opponent from scoring is almost as powerful as scoring itself. Also, many teams find it is easier to consistently do a good job in defending the shot than hitting them—they are "defense first" teams.

Therefore, the metrics for field goal shooting defense mirror those for offense.

Ball Handling

One of the age-old fundamentals of basketball offense is "taking care of the ball." While this entails many responsibilities, there are two that are preached by every coach at every level. One responsibility is passing the ball to find the best shot. Teams that do this have higher field goal percentages and more scoring consistency. Total assists are the most reliable measure of this effort.

The second responsibility is to avoid turnovers. A turnover not only deprives a team of an opportunity to score, it gives the opponent an additional opportunity to score. Scoring services are increasingly reporting "points off turnovers" as a more direct measure of the impact of turnovers.

Of course, many teams work hard to make their opponents' ball handling a liability, rather than a strength – it is key part of playing good defense. Limiting assists by disrupting an opponent's normal offensive plays and creating turnovers are signs of good defense.

The power of forcing a high turnover margin is demonstrated by Temple during the 2004-2005 season.

	FG Attempts	FG Pct.	Rebounds	Turnovers
Temple	1,714	38.9%	1083	293
Opponent	1,570	40.1%	1082	408
Margin	144	-1.2%	1	117

Temple had no rebounding margin, but took 144 more shots than its opponents. These shooting opportunities were largely attributable to an outstanding +117 turnover margin. Since Temple's excellence in defense was only exceeded by its horrid shooting, the extra shots were extremely valuable in gaining a margin of victory and/or keeping games close.

Assists and turnovers are commonly discussed in the same breath, and the assists-to-turnover ratio (ATO) is a popular stat. While there is some positive relationship between assists and turnovers, it is not necessarily strong or pervasive. As a result, it is preferable, when data is readily available, to look at the two separately. The relevant measures are "average turnovers" (the average number of turnovers per game when a team has the ball), "turnover margin" (the average difference per game between giving up the ball and getting the ball on turnovers) and "average assists" (the average number of assists per game).

The point guard is responsible for running the team on the floor and controlling the ball. A competent point guard is a minimum condition for team success, and a truly extraordinary point guard can propel his team deep into the NCAA Tournament. In evaluating point guards, assists, turnovers and ATO are all relevant and the key quantitative metrics of performance. While point guard scoring and rebounding are valued, they are considered bonuses relative to the basic job of protecting the ball and setting up teammates for high-percentage shots. ATO is much more relevant for point guards than entire teams.

Rebounds

Rebounding is important because it provides the means of increasing possessions, which in turn increases the number of shots a team gets and minimizes opponents' scoring opportunities. Additionally, offensive rebounds are even more valuable since a high proportion of them lead to high-percentage field goal attempts.

The most reliable measure of rebounding is "rebounding margin" which indicates the potential difference in shots generated from rebounding. This is more useful than number of rebounds, since, in some measure, the number of rebounds simply reflects a style of play. For example, a team that plays a deliberate half-court game will generally have fewer rebounds than a team that plays a wide-open running game. However, either team may give up more rebounds than it pulls down, thereby giving an advantage to opponents.

Modest rebound margins are not particularly meaningful. However, an average margin of at least four is significant. For example, in the 2003-2004 season, Fordham averaged 31.4 rebounds per game—a somewhat meaningless statistic without proper context. However, it had a -9.3 rebounding margin—opponents killed the Rams on the boards. Fordham was out-rebounded in 21 of 27 games. But all five Fordham wins that season were included in the six games in which it had a positive rebounding margin. Fordham lost every game in which it was out-rebounded.

Rebounding margin is no longer highly correlated with frontcourt size. At one time it was possible to anticipate a rebounding margin by looking at the rosters of the two teams to find out how big the frontcourt starters were. Increasingly, there are agile smaller frontcourt players that are excellent rebounders because of positioning and jumping skills, rather than size. Also, more teams have guards go to the boards to place more pressure on the defense.

Free Throws

The ability of a team to draw more fouls than it commits can translate into a significant scoring advantage. A free throw attempt margin translates into scoring margin. Plus, an opponent's foul troubles can force adjustments in the normal player rotations and key match-ups, which can lead to additional scoring benefits.

Some teams have a style of play that includes deliberately trying to create a free throw margin. Guards drive to the basket. Frontcourt players play a physical game. There are screens and picks to cause fouls as well as to create shots.

As with some other measures, modest free throw attempt margins are not material. However, an average margin of five or more is significant, and for most teams translates to three or four points extra points in the total score.

There is a tendency for the visiting team to commit more fouls than the home team. Frequently, this is attributed to a home court advantage, such as the officials being subconsciously subject to the will of the crowd. The real cause may be that for a variety of reasons the home team wins more often and losing teams, wherever they play, have a tendency to commit more fouls.

Regardless of the reason, the differences can be quite material. Wisconsin was the 2003-2004 regular-season Big Ten champion. All six of its losses were on the road. In each of the six games, the home opponent had more free throw attempts than Wisconsin. For the entire season, Wisconsin had an average free throw attempt margin of +6 per game. Excluding the six losses, Wisconsin had more free throw attempts than its opponent in 21 of 24 games.

Team Depth

A team's depth is defined by its talent and playing rotation. Most coaches have a set rotation with designated starters and reserves. It is not necessary to understand all of the details of a team's rotation or player match-ups in a specific game. Most important is each player's average minutes per game, as the players getting the most minutes are going to determine a team's performance.

Team depth is commonly defined as the number of players who average more than 10 minutes per game. An average of 10 minutes per game indicates that a player has a defined role and is called upon to play that role in most games. This is a gross metric that is sufficient for handicapping. However, you should recognize that it is subject to some distortion when some players on good teams get a lot of minutes in mop-up roles, when a player is frequently injured but gets 10 minutes a game when he plays, or a team has experimented with lots of starting lineups, and as a result, over the season, playing minutes have been widely distributed.

At the highest level there are four situations regarding team depth that you will encounter in evaluating a game. They are defined by a two-by-two matrix.

When both teams are deep, depth plays no significant role in forecasting a game's outcome. When both teams have little depth, it can affect the outcome for either team. To see how much of a factor depth might be you should look at secondary measures such as free throw attempt margins as an indicator of potential foul trouble.

Team A **High Depth**	Advantage Team A	Depth No Factor
Team A **Low Depth**	Secondary Factors Determine Advantage	Advantage Team B
	Team B **Low Depth**	**Team B** **High Depth**

The more significant situations are the ones in which one team has depth and the other team does not. In these situations, deep teams try to use their depth to wear out the opponent. They may press the length of the court, substitute frequently to maintain fresh legs, and actively try to draw fouls. Teams without depth recognize it and have playing styles that do not rely on bench strength. Nevertheless, depth mismatches usually work to the advantage of the team that is deeper.

10. Search for consistency in meaningful measures of performance.

Consistency is a beautiful thing! The risk of a wager diminishes when a team can be relied upon to perform in certain ways against certain types of opponents.

Consistency is not obvious and averages can be deceiving. After 10 games, two teams can have identical three-point shooting percentages of 35%. One may have achieved that average by hitting 50% of its shots in each of five games and 20% in each of the other five games. The other team may have achieved that average by hitting 35% of its shots in every game. While this is an extreme example, it shows how decomposing an average can provide insight about a team's performance. Not knowing whether a team will hit 50% or 20% of its attempts does not make a team more attractive to bet on.

While a team can demonstrate consistency in lots of things, there are four areas that are of particular importance in making wagering decisions. It is valuable to invest some extra time to assess a team's consistency.

- *Scoring Defense*—Teams have the ability to play very good defense almost every night. It requires focus, conditioning, and intelligence—attributes that players can always bring to the court. Many teams make defense the foundation of their game strategy. They expect fewer defensive "off-nights" than offensive "off-nights". The ability of a team to consistently hold down opponents' scoring and two- and three-point field goal percentages are comforting things to rely on when wagering.

- *Three-Point Shooting*—The percentage of all shots taken from behind the arc has been increasing. Three-point shots account for a high percentage of total scoring. Three point shots are harder to make than two point shots and teams have less consistency in shooting from behind the arc. Therefore, teams that "live by the three and die by the three" are worrisome unless they show that, almost regardless of the opponent, they can consistently hit a relatively high percentage of their three-point shots.

- *Scoring Balance*— It's worrisome to be dependent on a single big-time scorer. Coaches and bettors sometimes bestow their trust and part of their bankroll on a 20-year-old scoring stud. However, the better bet is the team that has four or five players averaging at least 10 points per game. The obvious advantage is that such a team is less vulnerable to an off night by a single player, systematically works for the best shots, is more difficult to defend, is less susceptible to foul trouble and has an advantage should the game go to overtime. Therefore, you should look at the number of players with scoring averages exceeding 10 points per game, and if time permits, look at how often at least three players score in double figures.

- *Turnovers*—Consistently low turnovers implies consistently good ball control. It means that a team generally has an opportunity to run its offense and to take its average number and selection of shots. Also, low turnovers result in fewer shooting opportunities for the opponent, and therefore less scoring. It is particularly reassuring when a team has low turnovers even when it is playing aggressive pressing teams.

To extend the turnover analysis of Temple described in Subsection 8, the team not only had a very low turnover average prior to post-season play (9.56), but it consistently took care of the ball. In 25 regular season games, Temple never committed more than 15 turnovers. The chart below shows the incidence of turnovers in those games. Similarly, Temple consistently gained a substantial turnover margin. On average, Temple committed only 76% of the turnovers committed by its opponents and was remarkably consistent in doing so. In 22 of 25 games Temple had a positive turnover margin. In 11 of its games Temple forced more than twice the number of turnovers than it committed (ratio <.5).

Turnovers	Games
0-5	2
6-10	16
11-15	7
16-20	0
Average = 9.56	

Turnover Ratio (Temple/ Opponent)	Games
0 - .50	11
.51 – 1.00	11
>1.00	3
Average = .76	

11. The Synthesis of Analysis: Selecting a Team

Determining the team to wager on is where basketball knowledge and judgment come into play. You will have conducted your analyses and looked at performance metrics, presumably focusing only on those things that might be important. Ultimately, you must isolate the areas where there are meaningful differences between the teams and decide how meaningful those differences are relative to the point spread.

Unfortunately, there is no mechanical way of determining exactly how much advantage you have relative to the point spread. It is not as easy as adding up a few numbers and getting an answer. There is as much judgment as quantitative analysis.

A systematic way of approaching this decision, which is demonstrated in detail in Chapter 4, is comprised of a three-level hierarchy of factors that forecast the outcome of the game.

- *Evaluating Recent Performance Against the Point Spread.* This entails an analysis of cover margins for each team, as well as simply looking at wins and losses against the point spread. Only significant positive or negative trends should be considered material. However, a major trend with respect to cover margins should be very highly weighted in forecasting game outcomes.

- *Assess Performance Against Comparable Opponents.* Compare the performance metrics for each team that were generated against comparable opponents. This would include field goal shooting, ball handling, free throw attempts, and rebounds. You should identify major differences between the two teams that indicate how the game is likely to be played and its outcome.

- *Assessment of Other Factors.* There are factors that validate the conclusions that might be reached from looking at comparables, and also represent game-specific conditions to be considered. These factors are very material, and in combination can carry as much weight as the analyses described above.

  o *Home vs.* Away—Indications of particular strength or weakness at home or on the road that help calibrate the home court advantage. This can be very material when the majority of your wagering competitors assume that the home court advantage is always four points.

o *Trends*—The extent to which the previous three or four games indicate meaningful changes in play that are likely to be perpetuated, thereby diminishing the value of the statistics from play in games earlier in the season that are relied on by many of your competitors.

o *Consistency*—The degree to which each team demonstrates consistency when playing comparable opponents and the extent to which averages can be relied on to forecast performance. If there is variability of play, it is worthwhile to search for an explanation.

o *Scoring Balance*—The degree to which scoring is distributed among the players for the two teams relative to the stringency of their defenses.

o *Depth* – The relative depth of the two teams and identification of those situations in which differences may have an impact on strategy and performance.

o *Special Conditions*—Game-specific conditions that could affect outcomes, but generally did not exist in prior games.

As will be shown in Chapter 4, you can systematically assess these factors and boil down the analysis to a "scorecard" that should support your wagering decision.

Remember, sometimes your forecast of the outcome of the game will be very different than the point spread, and at other times it will not. You should maintain objectivity and be sure that you don't imagine an advantage that doesn't really exist.

12. *Shopping for the best wagering terms has an impact on results.*

Getting the best terms on your wagers makes a big difference in the amount of money that you win. While most bettors would acknowledge that getting the best terms is always desirable, few appreciate how much difference it makes between winning and losing for the person who is wagering for both entertainment and to make money. It doesn't seem like getting an extra point or half point would make much of a difference, but it does.

For serious investors who only wager to make money, getting the extra half point is desirable but not critical to winning. These bettors are only wagering on games in which they think they have found a big advantage—the outcome that they forecast is a lot different than the actual point spread. If they think a spread should be 10 but it is only four, they will place the wager. If the spread becomes 4.5 or five, they will still place the wager, and their advantage will be modestly diminished. The small change in the point spread does not affect whether the wager is placed. It may slightly affect the amount wagered, and, on occasion, make the difference between winning and losing.

However, if you are wagering for entertainment as well as making money you will first select the games that you are interested in primarily for entertainment. Then you forecast the outcome and figure out how much advantage there is relative to the point spread. You will find yourself wagering on many games in which the advantage is very modest. When there is only a modest advantage—say two points relative to the prevailing spread—the difference of a half point is meaningful. When there is only a two point difference, a half-point can increase or decrease your advantage by 25% (.5/2 = 25%). Therefore, the half point means more to you than the professional college basketball investor.

There are two aspects of "shopping" for the best point spreads.

You should place your wager at a sports book that has the most favorable terms—the moneyline and point spread. First, you should check the moneylines and point spreads at the sports books with which you have accounts. However, while you might have accounts with only a few sports books, there are dozens of others that post their point spreads. There are websites that show reasonably current point spreads for many sports books. Consulting one of these sites gives you a comprehensive view of the market and enables you to see if any sports books have more favorable terms. If there are many that do, it may be likely that the point spread will move to your favor at the sports books with which you have accounts. It may be worth waiting awhile before placing the wager

Second, the closing point spread is generally different than the opening point spread. The terms of your point spread wager depend on when you place it. In some cases you might be able to anticipate the movement of the point spread and then place your wager accordingly. That takes time, and for a specific game, a level of sophistication found largely among professional college basketball investors. However, there are several rules of thumb that you should keep in mind.

If you think you have spotted a big advantage relative to the point spread, it is better to wager sooner than later. If there is truly a big advantage it will diminish over time as others spot it and place similar wagers. Even if many others don't spot it, those that do will place larger wagers that will diminish the advantage. In the worst case the point spread might get a little better, but once you have spotted a big advantage you have more to lose than to gain from waiting before placing your wager.

Also, just because a spread moves a half point in your favor is no reason to automatically increase your wager. As noted above, half points do make a big difference, but most people are not able to accurately calibrate their wagers to reflect small changes in point spreads. There is too great a tendency to magnify the impact of a half point movement in your favor and to wager more than is justified. Most of the time, it is better to be satisfied with your half-point windfall and to not increase the amount that you wager.

It should be emphasized that it takes little time to do basic spread shopping—only a fraction of the time that you may have spent handicapping the game and determining which team to wager on and how much money to place at risk. As a result, the return on investment from the time you spend shopping for point spreads may be as high as any other activity in the wagering process.

13. *Understanding the outcome of every wager.*

Wagering is not simply about winning and losing. It is also about why the outcome was what it was. By finding out why you won or lost you will improve your handicapping skills and become less susceptible to psychological traps.

Win or lose, the most important thing to find out after the wager is settled is whether you handicapped the game properly. There are a lot of things that affect the outcome of a game—it is outside your control. However, handicapping is within your control. An acceptable outcome is doing a good job in handicapping the game and making the right wager, but losing because the teams did not play to form. That is quite different than losing because you did a poor job of handicapping the game and never had much chance of winning. While you will be doing well if you win 60% of your wagers, you should satisfy yourself that 80% of the time you have made the right wager.

Handicapping is like consistent defense by college basketball teams. You can do a good job almost every night, and it will help you win a lot of games, but it won't enable you to win every game.

Even when you lose, knowing that you placed the right bet helps maintain confidence. Confidence is a critical element of college basketball wagering that can be maintained despite losses. On the other hand, when you have handicapped poorly, there is something to be learned. You have lost some money so you might as well get extra value by absorbing the lessons from a poor wager.

As noted earlier, selecting games on which to wager based on your desire to watch or listen to them tends to limit your unit win rate and the return on your bankroll. However, there is one major advantage of doing so. When you watch or listen to the game that you have wagered on you know, in detail, what happened. While box scores are very useful, you will have more insight about the game than that provided by the numbers.

4. Game Handicapping—A Step-By-Step Approach

There is a basic conflict in handicapping college basketball games: You would like to handicap games as thoroughly as possible to increase your chances of winning, yet you don't want to spend more time handicapping games than watching them. You don't want to spend lots of time handicapping a game only to find that there is little advantage relative to the point spread and only a modest wager is warranted.

The purpose of this handicapping methodology is to reconcile the typical handicapper's conflict. It has been developed to answer a common question among college basketball fans that enjoy wagering: If I only have a limited amount of time to handicap a game, what should I do and how should I best use my time?

The basic premise of this methodology is that if you spend about 20 minutes handicapping a game—about 10-15 minutes more than most fans already spend—you can achieve a unit win rate on your wagers of 60%. While spending even more time on each game will increase your win rate further, the payoff is not worth the effort unless you become a very serious investor in college basketball.

Also, once you become comfortable with this methodology and gain experience collecting data and conducting various analyses, you have the option of spending less time on each game or doing more analysis in the same amount of time and modestly increasing your win rate.

This approach has four important themes that ensure you make the best use of a limited amount of handicapping time.

- *Eliminate the Unpredictable Games Early.* There are indicators that the outcome of a game will be very difficult to forecast and that the probability is low that you will find a sizeable advantage. These indicators, such as a mismatch between teams and material injuries, are easy to identify. They provide a signal not to waste much time analyzing the game, and if you must wager, not to place much money at risk. You will be wagering primarily for entertainment.

- *Focus on Cause and Effect Relationships.* You do not have time, attention or emotional energy to look at enormous amounts of data or compute dozens of metrics for a game. You must focus on identifying cause and effect relationships and to always try to answer the question: How does a team play and why does it play that way? Fortunately, for most teams, only a handful of metrics and statistics in combination with knowledge of college basketball are needed to answer that question.

- *Collect Relevant Data Efficiently.* Ideally you will spend 80% of your time analyzing data and only 20% of your time collecting and manipulating it. The way to achieve that goal is first to know what data is needed to determine cause and effect relationships and then to identify reliable and easily accessible sources for it. It is very easy to rapidly load the data into spreadsheets programs that handle data manipulation and display. Let software do most of the work.

- *Quickly Find the Best Wagering Deal.* Once you know what team you want to wager on and how much to place at risk, it is important to quickly find the best deal—that is, the most favorable moneyline and the best point spread. Knowing where to look and acting decisively saves time and improves your win rate.

Six steps comprise the approach for efficiently handicapping college basketball games.

Step 1	Eliminate the Unpredictable Games Early
Step 2	Evaluate Recent Performance Against the Spread
Step 3	Assess Performance Against Comparable Opponents
Step 4	Assess Trends and Home vs. Away Advantage
Step 5	Assess Consistency, Personnel and Other Factors
Step 6	Draw Conclusions and Make Wagering Decision

Each of the six steps is described below. The discussion focuses on what to do and how to do it. There are frequent references to sections of Chapter 3 that addressed underlying principles and why certain types of analyses make sense.

To make this discussion more concrete, the handicapping approach is applied to a game played between UNC Charlotte and North Carolina State in the first round of the 2005 NCAA Tournament. The game was played on a neutral court in Syracuse.

The NCAA Tournament is tough to handicap and first round games provide the greatest challenge. If you can be a consistent winner when wagering on the NCAA Tournament, you can be extremely successful during the regular season. Using the UNC Charlotte vs. North Carolina State game as an example shows how you would apply the handicapping approach and the types of insights that you can gain from a focused analysis of two teams that on the surface appear to be similar.

Also, this game was deliberately chosen to illustrate how games do not always turn out the way that you have forecasted them. While the handicapping approach led to the right wagering decision and the chosen team covered, analyzing the game results indicates why it was a winning wager and where risk of losing was incurred.

You should make one adjustment because of the circumstances of the NCAA Tournament. You can ignore most of results of conference tournament games, paying attention only to exceptionally good and bad performances. There are too many unique circumstances of conference tournament play that can result in game outcomes that are misleading. For example, teams have different incentives. Some teams are already in the NCAA Tournament, while others are playing for their lives. Many conference tournament games are played on consecutive days. Such a schedule places a premium on depth, prevention of injury and preservation of energy. In some conferences a team must win four games in four days to become the tournament champion and gain an NCAA Tournament berth.

At the outset of handicapping a game, you should have three common types of information available.

- **Power Rating.** Any of the generally accepted power ratings are sufficient since they are only used to establish relative team strength within Division I. Sagarin's ratings are the most pervasive, appearing weekly in USA Today and on its website. Sagarin also provides the most thorough explanation of how the power ratings are determined and what they mean.

- **Game Logs.** A very good log will show the outcome of each game straight up, outcomes relative to the point spread and key statistics for each game related to shooting, ball handling and rebounding. There are good game logs at many websites, but you may need to manipulate the data from these sites to highlight the things that are most important to you. Figures 4-1 and 4-2 are examples of the typical game logs available for North Carolina State and Charlotte at the end of the regular season.

Game Handicapping—A Step-By-Step Approach

Figure 4-1: North Carolina State Team Log (2004-2005)

	Log										Offense			Defense		
Date	Site	Opponent	O P/R	Score	Line	Total	P/R	S/U	ATS	O/U	FG	FT	3pt	FG	FT	3pt
3/6/2005	H	Wake Forest	100.5	53-55	4	144	96.5	W	W	O	30-59	13-16	8-20	24-49	10-20	7-16
3/2/2005	A	Virginia	86	82-72	-3.5	141.5	95.5	W	W	O	24-51	26-38	10-20	25-59	16-23	6-21
2/26/2005	H	Virginia Tech	87.5	74-54	-10.5	134.5	94.5	W	W	U	24-49	15-22	10-22	17-45	15-26	5-12
2/22/2005	H	North Carolina	109.5	71-81	6.5	148.5	94.5	L	L	O	24-53	10-12	12-17	26-53	19-23	10-21
2/16/2005	H	Maryland	94	82-63	-2.5	150	93	W	W	U	25-57	19-21	13-30	21-57	16-22	5-15
2/13/2005	A	Georgia Tech	95.5	53-51	8.5	145	91.5	W	W	U	18-44	10-14	6-20	16-41	18-27	1-14
2/10/2005	A	Wake Forest	101	75-86	11.5	157.5	91	L	W	U	28-50	9-12	9-22	22-49	35-42	7-14
2/5/2005	H	Virginia	83	62-64	-11.5	152	93	L	L	O	18-45	21-29	5-20	20-43	20-24	6-21
2/3/2005	A	North Carolina	109	71-95	16	162	93	L	L	O	25-64	16-24	5-22	33-55	22-28	7-14
1/29/2005	A	Clemson	88.5	80-70	-1.5	135	91.5	W	W	O	27-43	13-21	13-20	27-60	11-21	5-18
1/26/2005	H	Florida State	87.5	64-70	-11.5	141	93.5	L	L	U	21-50	13-23	9-24	22-45	18-22	8-16
1/23/2005	A	Maryland	94.5	85-69	7	151	91.5	W	W	O	28-58	17-23	12-26	18-45	28-41	5-15
1/19/2005	A	Virginia Tech	82	71-72	-6	138	92	L	L	O	25-53	15-26	6-15	23-54	19-24	7-13
1/16/2005	H	Georgia Tech	98.5	76-68	1	143	91	W	W	O	19-50	30-37	8-20	27-59	12-19	2-13
1/13/2005	H	Duke	103	74-86	4	140	92	L	L	O	25-58	19-24	5-18	27-52	25-29	7-21
1/9/2005	A	Miami-Florida	88	66-67	-1.5	138.5	92	L	L	U	24-51	6-12	12-24	27-58	5-10	8-20
1/2/2005	H	West Virginia	92	69-82	-8.5	136	94	L	L	O	24-61	12-14	9-28	30-51	12-16	10-18
12/30/2004	A	St. John's	82.5	45-63	-14.5	138	96	L	L	U	13-65	17-22	2-24	25-57	12-17	1-7
12/28/2004	A	Columbia	72	84-74	-21.5	136	97.5	W	L	O	27-55	20-31	10-19	26-48	12-16	10-18
12/21/2004	A	BYU	83.5	72-61	-11	139	97.5	L	P	U	28-60	10-16	5-28	21-55	14-15	5-16
12/19/2004	A	Washington	94	64-68	5	163	97.5	L	W	U	26-64	7-10	5-23	27-60	12-21	2-13
12/15/2004	H	Louisiana-Lafayette	84.5	78-72	-19.5	142	99	W	L	O	21-42	29-44	7-22	26-60	11-21	9-17
12/11/2004	H	Liberty	69.5	94-60			99	W			35-75	15-19	9-23	24-60	7-13	5-20
12/5/2004	H	Manhattan	87.5	76-60	-17.5	137.5	99	W	L	U	30-59	11-19	5-18	20-61	15-20	5-16
11/29/2004	H	Purdue	87	60-53	-18	138	100.5	W	L	U	21-63	10-15	8-29	18-54	12-17	5-18
11/26/2004	H	Campbell	66.5	99-44			98.5	W			38-64	9-16	14-26	19-58	3-4	3-15
11/19/2004	H	East Carolina	83.5	100-66	-17	137	97	W	W	O	32-51	26-31	10-22	25-64	12-17	4-17
11/18/2004	H	Elon	73.5	71-45	-23	140	97	W	W	U	27-53	9-15	8-16	18-47	4-8	5-15
11/17/2004	H	New Orleans	80	92-58	-19.5	139	95.5	W	W	O	35-61	11-19	11-28	18-50	17-28	5-14

Source: Jim Feist College Basketball Stats

Figure 4-2: University of North Carolina -- Charlotte Team Log (2004-2005)

	Log			Results							Offense			Defense		
Date	Site	Opponent	O P/R	Score	Line	Total	P/R	S/U	ATS	O/U	FG	FT	3pt	FG	FT	3pt
3/5/2005	A	South Florida	80.5	73-85	-6.5	144.5	92	L	L	O	22-54	21-32	8-26	28-66	23-30	6-18
3/3/2005	A	Louisville	99.5	82-94	9.5	152	92	L	L	O	24-66	21-31	13-35	32-56	18-28	12-28
2/26/2005	H	So. Miss	72	81-58	-20	149	92	W	W	O	31-64	12-20	7-20	23-62	6-8	6-17
2/23/2005	H	Memphis	91	80-77	-5.5	146.5	92	W	L	O	25-55	22-35	8-16	29-61	10-15	9-23
2/19/2005	A	Tulane	73	86-67	-10	151.5	91.5	W	W	O	28-66	24-30	6-22	24-57	13-21	6-25
2/16/2005	H	DePaul	91	66-62	-6	143	91.5	W	L	U	24-67	16-22	2-19	22-58	10-11	9-22
2/12/2005	A	St. Louis	80	83-78*	-7	123	91.5	W	L	U	24-61	26-35	7-24	29-64	13-19	7-18
2/9/2005	H	Houston	86.5	91-71	-10.5	145	90	W	W	O	29-49	26-33	7-16	26-57	10-16	9-20
2/5/2005	H	Cincinnati	98.5	91-90	2.5	147	89	W	W	O	27-65	25-28	12-29	32-66	17-24	9-24
1/29/2005	A	East Carolina	77	51-54	-7	144.5	90.5	L	L	U	18-56	10-18	5-15	21-55	8-14	4-8
1/26/2005	H	TCU	83	94-87	-10.5	142	91	W	W	O	31-56	22-32	8-24	34-65	4-8	15-35
1/22/2005	A	Marquette	87	76-66	3.5	146	89.5	W	W	U	27-60	12-24	10-21	27-57	7-13	5-24
1/19/2005	A	Cincinnati	95.5	58-80	9	144.5	91	L	L	U	18-61	14-20	8-25	28-63	15-19	9-25
1/15/2005	H	St. Louis	78.5	65-59	-16	127	92.5	W	W	U	21-61	14-18	9-27	19-44	15-21	6-16
1/12/2005	A	Ala-Birmingham	91.5	91-85	3.5	158.5	91	W	W	O	31-61	20-26	9-20	32-73	14-18	7-27
1/8/2005	H	East Carolina	76.5	72-60	-15	140.5	92	W	L	O	26-64	15-23	5-18	27-59	4-9	2-14
12/29/2004	N	Central Connecticut	76	66-52	-12.5	150	92	W	W	U	24-61	12-16	6-22	20-57	7-12	5-18
12/28/2004	N	Yale	77	80-74	-13.5	160	93.5	W	W	U	31-68	8-11	9-19	30-61	7-11	7-19
12/22/2004	H	Indiana	88	74-73	-1.5	134.5	93.5	W	L	O	26-66	11-16	11-30	27-60	16-21	3-16
12/19/2004	H	NC Asheville	76.5	64-52			94.5	W			25-56	13-19	1-12	19-58	6-10	8-25
12/11/2004	H	Georgia State	80	80-65			94.5	W			24-65	27-39	5-21	25-61	9-11	7-27
12/8/2004	A	Davidson	83.5	87-68	-3	154	93	W	W	O	33-64	11-17	10-21	23-55	14-18	8-25
12/4/2004	H	Alabama	94	101-102*	-3	158.5	93	L	L	O	34-73	23-38	10-29	39-80	18-22	6-23
12/1/2004	H	Louisiana-Lafayette	87.5	84-68	-9.5	153	92	W	W	U	27-54	30-31	10-20	25-55	11-15	7-25
11/27/2004	A	Valparaiso	82	85-71			91	W			30-57	16-24	9-13	25-59	16-21	5-13
11/22/2004	H	Rutgers	88	71-73	-11.5	147	92	L	L	U	26-55	10-26	9-20	26-55	13-14	8-24
11/19/2004	H	Long Beach State	72	93-64	-23	148	91.5	W	W	O	31-58	20-29	11-21	22-70	17-20	3-25

Source: Jim Feist College Basketball Stats

- ***Team and Player Statistics.*** Cumulative season statistics for each player are important with respect to depth, scoring balance and other factors. Also, this information is frequently rolled up to show cumulative season statistics for the entire team and opponents. This information is readily available from ESPN, CBS SportsLine, Fox and other major media sites, plus just about every official team website. Figures 4-3 and 4-4 are examples of the player and team statistics for North Carolina State and Charlotte at the end of the season, including tournament play. Figures 4-5 and 4-6 are examples of commonly available rosters for each team.

Step 1: Eliminate the Unpredictable Games Early

The games on which you don't waste time handicapping or place substantial money at risk are as important as those that you do (Chapter 3, Section 4). So the first step in handicapping a game is to take a quick look at some key indicators to determine whether it is worth your attention.

A quick scan of Charlotte and North Carolina State indicated that the game was sufficiently predictable to justify a wager.

- The point spread favors North Carolina State by 4. This is not a mismatch. There are few plausible conditions under which coaching decisions might distort the final margin of victory such that a cover would become a non-cover and vice versa. If a team opens up a large lead and the coach decides to go to his bench, it could affect the ultimate margin of victory, but such a decision is unlikely to affect the outcome with respect to the point spread.

- While North Carolina State is favored by 4 points, it is the #10 seed in the region. Charlotte has a better seed at #7, but is the underdog. Also, the four-point spread corresponds to that calculated by several of the leading power ratings. These factors will not affect your analysis of the game, but they do affect the perceptions of the wagering public. These

Figure 4-3: North Carolina State -- Player Statistics (2004-2005)

Season Averages

NAME	GMS	MIN	PTS	REB	AST	TO	A/T	STL	BLK	PF	FG%	FT%	3P%	PPS
Iulius Hodge	34	34.6	17	6.6	4.8	2.6	1.8/1	1.4	0.7	2.2	0.493	0.668	0.255	1.44
Ilian Evtimov	35	30.4	9.8	3.8	2.1	2.1	1/1	1.2	0.1	3.1	0.447	0.667	0.426	1.36
Cameron Bennerman	29	23.1	9.6	2.7	1	1.2	1/1.2	0.8	0.2	1.6	0.475	0.732	0.393	1.36
Engin Atsur	35	32.6	9.4	2.6	2.5	1.2	2/1	1.6	0.1	2.6	0.406	0.768	0.383	1.22
Tony Bethel	27	25.6	8	3.8	2.5	1.6	1.6/1	1.5	0.1	2.1	0.414	0.773	0.336	1.25
Andrew Brackman	35	18.7	7.4	3.5	0.6	0.9	1/1.7	0.3	1.1	2	0.47	0.806	0.36	1.54
Jordan Collins	32	17.8	6.6	2.4	0.8	0.8	1/1	0.4	1	2.5	0.5	0.81	0.462	1.38
Gavin Grant	33	13.1	4.2	2.4	1.2	1.3	1/1.2	0.4	0.1	1.2	0.41	0.596	0.265	1.15
Levi Watkins	25	11.3	3.9	1.4	0.5	0.6	1/1.2	0.2	0.1	1.2	0.407	0.857	0.313	1.13
Cedric Simmons	31	10	3.5	1.8	0.5	0.7	1/1.6	0.2	1.1	1.9	0.506	0.545	0	1.3
Adam Simmons	1	3	0	1	0	1	-	0	0	0	0	0	0	-
Braxton Albritton	5	1	0	0	0	0.2	-	0	0	0	0	0	0	-
Will Roach	2	1	0	0	0.5	0	-	0	0	0.5	0	0	0	-
Team Averages	35	-	73.1	32	15.1	12.4	1.2/1	7.4	4.5	18.7	0.455	0.705	0.37	1.34

Figure 4-3: North Carolina State -- Player Statistics (2004-2005), cont.

Season Totals

NAME	GMS	MIN	FGM	FGA	FTM	FTA	3PM	3PA	PTS	OFF	DEF	TOT	AST	TO	STL	BLK	PF
Julius Hodge	34	1177	197	400	169	253	14	55	577	85	140	225	162	89	48	24	75
Ilian Evtimov	35	1064	113	253	52	78	66	155	344	31	102	133	73	74	41	5	110
Engin Atsur	35	1141	110	271	43	56	67	175	330	21	71	92	86	43	57	5	92
Cameron Bennerman	29	670	97	204	41	56	42	107	277	28	50	78	29	36	24	7	46
Andrew Brackman	35	655	79	168	83	103	18	50	259	53	71	124	20	33	12	40	69
Tony Bethel	27	691	72	174	34	44	39	116	217	21	82	103	68	43	41	2	56
Jordan Collins	32	569	76	152	34	42	24	52	210	34	43	77	26	26	13	33	80
Gavin Grant	33	432	50	122	31	52	9	34	140	20	58	78	38	44	13	2	39
Cedric Simmons	31	309	42	83	24	44	0	2	108	23	34	57	14	23	5	35	59
Levi Watkins	25	282	35	86	12	14	15	48	97	9	26	35	12	14	6	3	29
Adam Simons	1	3	0	1	0	0	0	0	0	1	0	1	0	1	0	0	0
Braxton Albritton	5	5	0	0	0	0	0	0	0	0	0	0	0	1	0	0	0
Will Roach	2	2	0	1	0	0	0	1	0	0	0	0	1	0	0	0	1
Team Totals	**35**	**-**	**871**	**1915**	**523**	**742**	**294**	**795**	**2559**	**375**	**746**	**1121**	**529**	**435**	**260**	**156**	**656**

Source: ESPN

Note: Includes results for all games, including conference and NCAA Tournament

Figure 4- 4: University of North Carolina--Charlotte -- Player Statistics (2004-2005)

Season Averages

NAME	GMS	MIN	PTS	REB	AST	TO	A/T	STL	BLK	PF	FG%	FT%	3P%	PPS
Curtis Withers	28	32.4	18	8.1	1.8	3	1/1.7	1.1	0.9	3.1	0.468	0.662	0.423	1.34
Eddie Basden	29	36.2	15.2	8.4	3.7	2.6	1.4/1	3.2	0.1	2	0.487	0.724	0.386	1.39
Brendan Plavich	29	32.8	13.7	2.7	1.7	1.4	1.1/1	1	0.1	1.3	0.379	0.618	0.388	1.21
E.J. Drayton	29	22.8	8.7	4.6	1.2	1.4	1/1.1	0.5	0.2	2.4	0.367	0.779	0.353	1.26
Mitchell Baldwin	28	30.4	7.5	2.9	3.8	1.6	2.4/1	1.3	0.1	1.5	0.468	0.774	0.233	1.5
Leemire Goldwire	29	16.7	6.2	1.9	1.3	1.1	1.2/1	0.8	0	1.9	0.349	0.677	0.348	1.06
Martin Iti	29	18.2	5	4	0.5	1.2	1/2.4	0.3	1.7	2.4	0.512	0.319	0	1.14
Chris Nance	28	13.4	4.1	3.3	0.2	0.9	1/5.2	0.4	0.1	2.2	0.451	0.702	0	1.26
Chris Sager	22	3.6	0.6	0.3	0.1	0.2	1/1.7	0.1	0	0.2	0.267	0.667	0.231	0.87
Travis Gordon	7	1.3	0	0.1	0	0.1	-	0	0	0.3	0	0	0	-
Tripp Miller	5	1	0	0	0.2	0	-	0	0	0.2	0	0	0	-
Team Averages	**29**	**-**	**77.8**	**38.6**	**14.1**	**13.4**	**1.1/1**	**8.7**	**3.2**	**17**	**0.432**	**0.684**	**0.368**	**1.28**

Figure 4-4: University of North Carolina--Charlotte -- Player Statistics (2004-2005), cont.

Season Totals

NAME	GMS	MIN	FGM	FGA	FTM	FTA	3PM	3PA	PTS	OFF	DEF	TOT	AST	TO	STL	BLK	PF
Curtis Withers	28	908	175	374	131	198	22	52	503	96	132	228	49	83	31	25	88
Eddie Basden	29	1049	155	318	110	152	22	57	442	76	169	245	108	76	93	4	58
Brendan Plavich	29	951	125	330	34	55	114	294	398	7	72	79	48	42	30	3	39
E.J. Drayton	29	662	73	199	81	104	24	68	251	54	80	134	36	40	15	6	71
Mitchell Baldwin	28	852	66	141	72	93	7	30	211	22	60	82	107	45	36	2	43
Leemire Goldwire	29	484	59	169	21	31	40	115	179	14	42	56	39	33	23	0	55
Martin Iti	29	527	65	127	15	47	0	0	145	57	59	116	14	34	10	48	71
Chris Nance	28	374	41	91	33	47	0	0	115	43	50	93	5	26	11	4	61
Chris Sager	22	79	4	15	2	3	3	13	13	3	3	6	3	5	3	0	4
Travis Gordon	7	9	0	3	0	0	0	1	0	0	1	1	0	1	0	0	2
Tripp Miller	5	5	0	1	0	0	0	0	0	0	0	0	1	0	0	0	1
Team Totals	**29**	**-**	**763**	**1767**	**499**	**730**	**232**	**630**	**2257**	**420**	**699**	**1119**	**409**	**389**	**252**	**92**	**493**

Source: ESPN
Note: Includes results for all games, including conference and NCAA Tournament

Figure 4-5 North Carolina State   Roster (2004-2005)

NUM	NAME	POS	HT	WT	CLASS	HOMETOWN
3	Ilian Evtimov	F	6-7	232	Junior	Winston-Salem, NC
4	Will Roach	F	6-5	201	Senior	Raleigh, NC
10	Braxton Albritton	G	6-1	212	Freshman	Raleigh, NC
11	Gavin Grant	G-F	6-7	190	Freshman	Bronx, NY
13	Cameron Bennerman	G-F	6-4	198	Junior	Greensboro, NC
14	Engin Atsur	G	6-3	200	Sophomore	
21	Levi Watkins	F	6-8	235	Senior	Rockville, MD
22	Tony Bethel	G	6-2	178	Junior	Fort Washington, MD
24	Julius Hodge	G-F	6-7	205	Senior	Harlem, NY
32	Jordan Collins	C	6-10	242	Senior	Hyattsville, MD
33	Cedric Simmons	F-C	6-9	216	Freshman	Shallotte, NC
40	Andrew Brackman	F	6-10	205	Freshman	Cincinnati, OH

Source: ESPN

Figure 4-6 University of North Carolina -- Charlotte   Roster (2004-2005)

NUM	NAME	POS	HT	WT	CLASS	HOMETOWN
0	Chris Nance	F	6-8	250	Junior	Ft. Lauderdale, FL
1	E.J. Drayton	F	6-8	215	Junior	Charlotte, NC
2	Martin Iti	C	7-0	240	Sophomore	
3	Curtis Withers	F	6-8	230	Junior	Charlotte, NC
5	Brendan Plavich	G	6-2	207	Senior	Dalton, GA
10	Jerrell Lewis	G	6-2	195	Freshman	Brooklyn, NY
12	Leemire Goldwire	G	6-1	180	Freshman	Palm Beach Gardens,
13	Eddie Basden	F	6-5	205	Senior	Washington, DC
14	Tripp Miller	F	6-8	220	Junior	Denver, NC
20	Mitchell Baldwin	G	6-2	190	Junior	Rural Hall, NC
21	Chris Sager	G	6-4	180	Senior	Waukesha, WI
50	Travis Gordon	G	6-4	190	Sophomore	Richfield, NC

Source: ESPN

mixed signals in the market—the point spread relative to the seeding—could create a defective line and a wagering advantage for bettors who do some homework and are not concerned about this seeming anomaly.

- The game will be played in Syracuse, New York. This is a standard venue for big-time basketball. Both teams are used to playing in front of large crowds. There is no reason to think that the fans attending the game will overwhelmingly support one team over the other. Syracuse is truly a neutral site.

- There is uncertainty regarding the availability of Tony Bethel and Jordon Collins of North Carolina State. They missed much of the ACC Tournament with injuries. Despite their absence, North Carolina State played very well and used its success in that tournament to qualify for the NCAA Tournament. While both players are expected to get playing time against Charlotte, the real question is whether their absence substantially diminishes the predictability of this game.

  Even without Collins and Bethel, North Carolina State has seven players who have averaged more than 12 minutes per game during the season. North Carolina State is well rested for this game, so a slightly short bench should not affect the outcome. Finally, North Carolina State clearly worked out an effective rotation in its three ACC Tournament games. While uncertainty regarding the availability of Bethel and Collins might moderate the amount wagered on the game, it is nevertheless a game worth handicapping and wagering on.

The overall conclusion of the initial scan of this game is to proceed to Step 2 of the handicapping process.

Step 2: Evaluate Recent Performance Against the Spread

The best single indicator of whether a team is improving or deteriorating relative to the perceptions of the wagering public is the average margin by which the team covers or fails to cover, as well as the frequency of each occurrence. (See Chapter 3, Section 6).

The simple logic is that if a team not only covers but consistently blows away the point spread, that team is consistently undervalued by the wagering public. Similarly, a team that not only fails to cover, but, on average, fails to cover by a lot, is getting more respect from the wagering public than it deserves. If the wagering public consistently has had a team pegged wrong for awhile, it is unlikely to make a major correction in the immediate game.

This is an easy analysis to conduct, but it is generally less obvious among the wagering public because the average cover and non-cover margins are not readily available at websites. This is an example of a metric that you need to construct from available data, but it does not take long and has high value. Figures 4-7 and 4-8 display the cover margins against the spread for North Carolina State and Charlotte, respectively.

North Carolina State does very well against the point spread, both in terms of covering and cover margin. Charlotte is inconsistent against the point spread—there are no meaningful trends or tendencies, except perhaps a susceptibility to letdowns against lesser teams.

North Carolina State was 7-3 ATS in its last 10 games of the regular season. The team covered by an average of 7.85, including two games against Wake Forest and games against Maryland and Georgia Tech. In the three games in which North Carolina State did not cover, it failed by an average of 8.33. However, two of those games were against North Carolina—a superior team, an arch rival, and a highly ranked and highly seeded team.

Additionally, it should be noted that in the ACC Tournament, North Carolina State covered and won its games in the first and second rounds against Florida State and Wake Forest with an average cover margin of 14. It lost and failed to cover against Duke by only one point relative to the point spread in the third round.

Figure 4-7 Performance Against the Spread and Cover Margin -- North Carolina State

| | Log | | | | | Results | | | |
Date	Site	Opponent	Score	Line	Outcome	Margin	P/R	S/U	ATS
3/6/2005	H	Wake Forest	53-55	4	2	-2	96.5	W	W
3/2/2005	A	Virginia	82-72	-3.5	-10	-6.5	95.5	W	W
2/26/2005	H	Virginia Tech	74-54	-10.5	-20	-9.5	94.5	W	W
2/22/2005	H	North Carolina	71-81	6.5	10	3.5	94.5	L	L
2/16/2005	H	Maryland	82-63	-2.5	-19	-16.5	93	W	W
2/13/2005	A	Georgia Tech	53-51	8.5	-2	-10.5	91.5	W	W
2/10/2005	A	Wake Forest	75-86	11.5	11	-0.5	91	L	W
2/5/2005	H	Virginia	62-64	-11.5	2	13.5	93	L	L
2/3/2005	A	North Carolina	71-95	16	24	8	93	L	L
1/29/2005	A	Clemson	80-70	-1.5	-10	-8.5	91.5	W	W

Figure 4-8 Performance Against the Spread and Cover Margin -- UNC-Charlotte

Date	Log		Results				
	Site	Opponent	Score	Line	Outcome	Margin	S/U	ATS
3/5/2005	A	South Florida	73-85	-6.5	8	14.5	L	L
3/3/2005	A	Louisville	82-94	9.5	12	2.5	L	L
2/26/2005	H	So. Miss	81-58	-20	-23	-3	W	W
2/23/2005	H	Memphis	80-77	-5.5	-3	2.5	W	L
2/19/2005	A	Tulane	86-67	-10	-19	-9	W	W
2/16/2005	H	DePaul	66-62	-6	-4	2	W	L
2/12/2005	A	St. Louis	83-78*	-7	-5	2	W	L
2/9/2005	H	Houston	91-71	-10.5	-20	-9.5	W	W
2/5/2005	H	Cincinnati	91-90	2.5	-1	-3.5	W	W
1/29/2005	A	East Carolina	51-54	-7	3	10	L	L

In contrast, Charlotte went 4-6 ATS in its last ten games. In the four games in which it covered, the average cover margin was 6.25—largely against lesser competition. Coincidentally, the average failure to cover was also 6.25. However, looking at the average margins in games in which Charlotte failed to cover tells an important story. In four of the games it failed to cover by only two or 2.5 points—the other two were bad straight up losses to South Florida and East Carolina. Overall, this indicates that the wagering public largely has Charlotte pegged accurately. Charlotte has no particular trends or tendencies that are pertinent to this game.

Step 3: Assess Performance Against Comparable Opponents

Performance against comparable teams in the recent past is a good indicator of likely performance in this game. The two best indicators of comparability are overall team strength, as indicated by well-accepted power ratings, and style of play. The former is easy to ascertain; the latter is more difficult. However, in general, how a team plays against much better and much worse opponents should not have much bearing on your assessment of the game. (See Chapter 3, Section 8)

Using the Feist ratings, North Carolina State and Charlotte finished the season with power ratings of 96 and 92, respectively. Interestingly, the difference in these power ratings precisely matches the point spread for the game. This type of situation, particularly when Charlotte is the higher seed, highlights a key issue: Do power ratings have an exceptional ability to anticipate the point spread in the market? Or do the major power ratings substantially affect the perceptions of casual bettors and help move the point spread toward that calculated by the ratings?

As shown below, using the Feist power ratings, there were seven comparable teams played by North Carolina State since January 15, 2005, with an average power rating of 91.7

Figure 4-9: Comparable Opponents of North Carolina State

Date	Site	Opponent	Power Rating
2/26/2005	H	Virginia Tech	87.5
2/16/2005	H	Maryland	94
2/13/2005	A	Georgia Tech	95.5
1/29/2005	A	Clemson	88.5
1/26/2005	H	Florida State	87.5
1/23/2005	A	Maryland	94.5
1/16/2005	H	Georgia Tech	98.5
		Average	91.7

Charlotte's strength is comparable to the teams in the middle of the pack in the ACC. Also, it is fairly clear that during the conference season North Carolina State plays a steady diet of teams of the general quality of Charlotte. Notably, the games against Wake Forest, North Carolina and Duke during this six week period were excluded. Those teams are substantially better than Charlotte, and to include them would distort the analysis.

An element of comparability is style of play. Several of these teams replicate Charlotte's style—a strong inside-outside game in which quality three-point shooting is relied upon to open up the court. As importantly, there is nothing in Charlotte's approach to either offense or defense that is unique and requires unique preparation. Except for its obvious importance, North Carolina State can prepare for this game in the same way it prepares for other games against quality teams.

As shown in Figure 4-10, Charlotte played six opponents comparable to North Carolina State since January 12. These opponents were the best of Conference USA. There are no teams so superior to North Carolina State that they need to be excluded to avoid distorting the analysis. In fact, there were a reasonable number of games against lesser teams within and outside the conference which should have no bearing on this analysis, and were excluded.

Figure 4-10: Comparable Opponents of Charlotte

Date	Site	Opponent	Power Rating
3/3/2005	A	Louisville	99.5
2/23/2005	H	Memphis	91
2/16/2005	H	DePaul	91
2/9/2005	H	Houston	86.5
2/5/2005	H	Cincinnati	98.5
1/19/2005	A	Cincinnati	95.5
1/12/2005	A	Ala-Birmingham	91.5
		Average	94.5

In terms of style of play, these teams are not very similar to North Carolina State. Cincinnati relies on tough defense and scoring inside. Alabama-Birmingham relies on withering pressure and a very deep bench. Memphis and DePaul best replicate the style of North Carolina State, but are less skilled.

Performance Against the Spread

Once comparable opponents are identified, you should quickly check each team's performance against the spread and cover margin. The purpose is to see if there is any change in the results from Step 2 when the comparable opponents are isolated.

The results from Step 2 are fully confirmed, and, in fact, the differences between the teams are accentuated. Against comparable teams, Charlotte went 2-4 ATS. In four of the games there was only a small difference between the outcome of the game and the point spread. In contrast, against comparable opponents North Carolina State went 6-2 ATS with an average cover margin exceeding 12 points. In each of the six games that North Carolina State covered, it beat the spread by nine points or more. The two games that North

Carolina State failed to cover do not undermine the basic conclusion of increasing strength and being undervalued by the wagering public. There was a bad loss to Florida State on January 26 in which the failure to cover margin was 17.5 points, and a loss on January 9 at Miami (Florida) in which North Carolina State failed to cover by 2.5 points. These games were sufficiently early in the season to be only marginally relevant in handicapping this game.

Primary Statistics

Typically, there are two sets of statistics that you should isolate for games against comparable teams. (See Chapter 3, Section 9). The primary set is related to shooting—both on offense and defense. Shooting is typically the most important factor in team performance, and it is the most susceptible to the defensive skills and style of play of opponents. Statistics on shooting are readily available from many different sources, so there is only a modest amount of effort required to collect and display precisely the data needed for your analysis.

When the primary performance statistics for games with North Carolina State's five comparable opponents (seven games) are isolated, there are several important conclusions.

	Offense	Defense
Field Goal Pct.	46%	43%
2-Pt. Field Goal Pct.	47%	48%
3-Pt. Field Goal Pct.	45%	31%
Pct. 3-Pt Shots/Total	46%	30%

North Carolina State is tough on teams that shoot threes— a critical element of Charlotte's game. Limiting opponents to a 31% three-point shooting percentage is a particular advantage in this game. Opponents tend to work inside where North Carolina State might be a bit more vulnerable.

On offense North Carolina State tends to rely on the three—46% of all shots taken are threes—but it shoots well against the caliber of teams like Charlotte. Hitting 45% of three-point shots is truly exceptional against quality competition, and, as will be shown below, is higher than its rate against vastly superior teams and lesser teams.

In this case, the ability to hit threes leads to more three-point attempts—it is not the result of limited shooting capabilities or lack of offensive discipline. North Carolina State also shoots well from two-point range. To be successful, Charlotte will need to stop two-point as well as three-point shots. Charlotte will recognize this and have a game plan to stop both, but is there evidence that they have the capacity to do so?

Charlotte has not had much success against teams of the quality of North Carolina State. The shooting statistics against the six comparable opponents are as follows:

	Offense	Defense
Field Goal Pct.	40%	47%
2-Pt. Field Goal Pct.	42%	53%
3-Pt. Field Goal Pct	36%	39%
Pct. 3-Pt. Shots/ Total	38%	40%

Quality teams beat Charlotte at its own game by regularly hitting from behind the arc as well as inside. Allowing comparable opponents to hit 39% of their three-point shots is below average, and clearly encouraged those teams to take a higher percentage of their shots from behind the arc—40%. This susceptibility to the three is not a statistical fluke—every comparable opponent hit more than 36% of its threes. Despite a fairly strong inside game, Charlotte is highly susceptible from inside the arc as well. Allowing opponents to hit 53% of their two-point shots is not an admirable performance. There is an obvious conclusion: Defending the shot is not one of Charlotte's strengths.

Comparing these tendencies, the expectations for the North Carolina State vs. Charlotte game are:

- North Carolina State should be able to score. Should Charlotte choose to focus on stopping the three-point shot, North Carolina State is very capable of changing its offense to exploit Charlotte's porous 53% two-point field goal defense. Overall, Charlotte gives little indication of being able to contain North Carolina State's offense.

- Charlotte should have difficulty getting its offense in gear since there is a good chance that North Carolina State will shut down the three, then collapse on Charlotte's big men.

This game also illustrates the power of looking at comparable games rather than season averages. Statistics for season averages relative to only comparable games played by Charlotte are as follows:

	Offense		Defense	
	Comparables	Season	Comparables	Season
Field Goal Pct.	40%	43%	47%	44%
2-Pt. Field Goal Pct.	42%	47%	53%	50%
3-Pt. Field Goal Pct.	36%	37%	39%	32%
Pct. 3-Pt Shots/Total	38%	36%	40%	36%

Charlotte's offensive statistics for the season are only slightly better than those for opponents comparable to North Carolina State. Yet most opponents were of lesser strength. The bigger difference was on defense—three-point field goal defense, a particularly important factor in this game, is much better for the season than against comparable opponents. It is clearly a key factor in defeating lesser teams. Charlotte's overall season performance looks different than its performance against teams comparable to North Carolina State. This illustrates why relying on season averages can be misleading.

With respect to North Carolina State, there are some differences between its averages for the season and those for comparable games. Against comparable teams, North Carolina State shoots threes exceptionally well, and therefore takes more of them. Its two-point shooting percentage is lower against such teams, but that seems to reflect the relative efficiency of taking the three-point shot rather than lack of ability to hit from two-point range. At the same time, there are no material statistical differences in defensive averages for the season and comparable opponents. This indicates that as the schedule got tougher, the defense of North Carolina State improved. The season averages are significantly weighted by early season games against lesser competition such as New Orleans, East Carolina, Elon, Campbell, Liberty, Columbia, Manhattan and Purdue. Maintaining a strong defense, despite improving competition, is another sign of North Carolina State's improvement over the last six weeks of the regular season.

	Offense		Defense	
	Comparable	Season	Comparable	Season
Field Goal Pct.	46%	46%	43%	43%
2-Pt. Field Goal Pct.	47%	52%	48%	47%
3-Pt. Field Goal Pct.	45%	37%	31%	35%
Pct. 3-Pt Shots/Total	46%	42%	30%	31%

Secondary Performance Statistics

The second set of valuable team performance statistics that you should look at pertains to rebounding, ball handling and free throw attempts. These statistics are largely available or easily computed. Secondary performance statistics are valuable, so some effort at the outset of the season to find reliable sources of well-presented data is worthwhile.

With respect to secondary performance statistics, North Carolina State consistently does slightly better against teams comparable to Charlotte than its season averages. North Carolina State typically has a nice average turnover margin for the season (2.9) that, in fact, increases slightly against teams comparable to Charlotte (3.2). Also,

North Carolina State is excellent at moving the ball to attain high-percentage shots. It generates an average of 15.1 assists per game for the season, which increases to 15.6 against teams comparable to Charlotte. Most compelling is a very advantageous assist-to-turnover ratio for the entire season (1.2 vs. .8), which also increases against teams comparable to Charlotte (1.33 vs. .76). These are important team attributes that can generally be sustained in big games. They lead to higher scoring because of better shot selection on more shooting opportunities.

	Comparables	Season
Rebounding Margin	-1.3	-2.3
Avg. Turnovers	11.7	12.4
Avg. Assists	15.6	15.1
Assists-Turnover Ratio	1.33	1.2
Avg. Turnovers—Opponent	14.9	15.3
Avg. Turnover Margin	3.2	2.9
Assist-Turnovers Ratio—Opponent	.76	.8
Free Throw Attempt Margin	1.3	.4

In looking at Charlotte with respect to secondary performance statistics, there are few material differences between season averages and performance against comparable teams. Average turnovers per game are a bit lower (12.0 vs. 13.4), as are assists (11.8 vs. 14.1). The net effect is a diminished ATO ratio relative to comparable opponents (.99 vs. 1.11)

	Comparables	Season
Avg. Rebounding Margin	0	1.5
Avg. Turnovers	12.0	13.4
Avg. Assists	11.8	14.1
Assists-Turnover Ratio	.99	1.05
Avg. Turnovers—Opponent	14	16.2
Turnover Margin	2	2.8
Assist-Turnovers Ratio—Opponent	1.11	.91
Free Throw Attempt Margin	8.5	8

The comparisons to season averages for both teams, while interesting, do not yield much meaningful information that bears on the outcome of this game. Useful information is derived when the secondary statistics for Charlotte and North Carolina State are directly compared.

	NC State vs. Comparables	Charlotte vs. Comparables
Rebounding Margin	-1.3	0
Avg. Turnovers	11.7	12.0
Avg. Assists	15.6	11.8
Assists-Turnover Ratio	1.33	.99
Avg. Turnovers – Opponent	14.9	14
Avg. Turnover Margin	3.2	2
Assist-Turnovers Ratio – Opponent	.76	1.11
Free Throw Attempt Margin	1.3	8.5

There are several clear expectations for how this game will be played.

- Charlotte should gain an advantage in free throw attempts, as it has done throughout the season. This should help increase Charlotte's scoring by 3-5 points, and could conceivably create some depth problems for North Carolina State if Bethel and Collins do not play.

- North Carolina State is unlikely to be taken out of its ball movement offense that uses passing (i.e., assists) to create good shots. Charlotte struggles a bit against teams comparable to North Carolina State. It may have trouble achieving its desired shot selection.

- North Carolina State is also likely to attain a small turnover margin, but that should not have a material impact on the outcome of the game.

Step 4: Assess Trends and Home/Away Advantage

Steps 2 and 3 in this process enable you to identify strengths and weaknesses of the teams, forecast the outcome of the game, and develop preliminary conclusions regarding the team on which to wager and how much advantage there is relative to the point spread. Steps 4 and 5 provide a means of confirming your conclusions on the team on which to wager and to refine the calculation of advantage relative to the point spread.

The purpose of Step 4 is to stand back and consider the trends that both teams have shown during the season and, also, to assess whether there is likely to be any significant impact of the playing venue, in this case a neutral court (See Chapter 3, Sections 3 and 7).

Because of the strong competition in the ACC, it's hard to truly discriminate trends for teams in the middle of the pack. North Carolina State had a credible showing in the ACC Tournament. Prior to that, it had been playing reasonably well for about six weeks. In the last 10 regular season games, North Carolina State was 5-5, but the losses were to North Carolina (2), Wake Forest (2) and Virginia. North Carolina State's seemingly mediocre regular season record of 17-12 is distorted by five early losses (before January 15) to teams that turned out to be better than expected—Washington, Miami, West Virginia, Duke and St. John's. Those quality losses, plus losses against the elite of the ACC, cast North Carolina State in a better light.

When playing on a neutral court, a team's past performance on the road is the best indicator. North Carolina State is a road-tested team—most ACC arenas are hostile environments. Playing on a neutral court will not adversely affect North Carolina State. Since mid-January, North Carolina State went 4-3 on the road and 5-2 ATS. Every cover on the road during that period was convincing.

Charlotte started the season 12-2 against weak competition. There were no notable wins. The two losses were to Alabama and Rutgers. Since then, Charlotte went 9-4 (excluding the Conference USA Tournament) and 5-8 ATS. During this period, Charlotte lost more games that it should have won—to East Carolina, TCU, St. Louis and South Florida—than big wins. Its only major win was defeating Cincinnati at home. Overall, the market has adjusted to Charlotte's performance. Most of the recent lines have been accurate. While Charlotte's loss in its conference tournament may have awakened the team, it has not performed that well during the season and cannot be said to be playing its best basketball in mid-March.

Conference USA is a very creditable conference so Charlotte has very good road experience. Playing at Cincinnati, Louisville, Memphis and DePaul is not easy. However, the team's performance on the road is a bit suspect. Since mid-January, Charlotte has gone 3-4 straight up and 2-5 ATS on the road.

Overall, this step confirms the relative strength of North Carolina State. Charlotte does not have a positive season trend—it is not playing its best basketball now—and it does not play particularly well on the road. North Carolina State is peaking and is both comfortable and successful on the road.

Step 5: Assess Consistency, Personnel and Other Factors

This step seeks to do two things. First, it provides some insight into how likely each team is to perform to form—how likely it is that the teams will play the way you think they are going to play (See Chapter 3, Section 10). Second, by looking at the teams' personnel and some other factors, you can satisfy yourself that you understand why each team plays the way it does (See Chapter 3, Section 9). These analyses will more significantly affect how comfortable you are with the team you select and help calibrate the amount that you wager.

The specific things you should consider are the consistency of performance statistics – particularly defense, scoring balance, and depth—and special conditions. The results when Charlotte and North Carolina State are evaluated on these attributes are described below.

- *Statistical Consistency.* It is valuable to ensure that some of the key statistical averages for comparable games are not misleading and do not conceal erratic and unpredictable performance.

  With respect to North Carolina State, there is a level of consistency that is very reassuring. In comparable games, North Carolina State has an incredible 45% three-point field goal shooting percentage. Except for the game at Georgia Tech in which North Carolina State hit only 30% of those shots, it has exceeded 38% in the other seven comparable games. Similarly, North Carolina State not only shows a large average assist-to-turnovers advantage, it has had a better ATO than the opponent in all eight comparable games, and has forced more turnovers than it has committed in all but one game.

  The one area of concern for this game may be defending against the three-point shot. Comparable opponents have hit only 31% of their shots from behind the arc against North Carolina State. However, there is a relatively high degree of inconsistency. North Carolina State has had exceptional success against Georgia Tech, limiting it to 13% and 7% in their two meetings. However, the defensive three-point percentage against Virginia Tech, Florida State and Miami were 42%, 50% and 40%, respectively. This could imply defensive letdowns against lesser teams. Alternatively, it might imply that North Carolina State took advantage of Georgia Tech's season-long backcourt problems associated with the injury to B.J. Elder, an excellent three-point shooter (37.3% shooting accuracy in his first three seasons).

Charlotte's performance is interesting in that it shows both dangerous inconsistency and dangerous consistency. As indicated previously, three-point shooting will be important. Charlotte is relatively inconsistent against comparable opponents, despite an average of 36%. Charlotte hit only 11% against DePaul, but 50% and 45%, respectively, against Memphis and Alabama-Birmingham. Unfortunately, Charlotte has a defensive consistency. It is always vulnerable to the three-point shot. All comparable opponents have hit between 36% and 43% of their three-point shots—the 39% average for comparable opponents is truly representative. This is a big liability when matched with North Carolina State's consistency in hitting threes.

Charlotte is consistent in free throw attempts, generating a positive margin in all six games. Also, with one exception, Charlotte always turns the ball over less than its opponent. This confirms the expectation of some scoring margin created by free throws, and perhaps diminishes the expectation that North Carolina State will create a slight turnover margin.

- *Scoring Balance.* The more players on a team who have double-digit scoring averages, the more reliable the team's scoring. Teams with three or more double-digit scorers are less susceptible to gimmick defenses, injuries and off-nights. In contrast, when there are only one or two scorers, the fate of the game and frequently your wager rests in their hands.

In this game, North Carolina State presents an interesting situation. There is no doubt that North Carolina State is dependent on the scoring of Julius Hodge, who averaged 17 points per game during the regular season. Among the rest of the team, however, scoring is balanced with five players averaging 7-10 points per game. Virtually everyone on the team shoots threes, so North Carolina State's strongest advantage should be reliably applied in this game. Nevertheless, North

Carolina State is vulnerable if Charlotte can stop Hodge. As important as his scoring totals is that he is the go-to guy when North Carolina State needs a basket. Some of the scoring balance is achieved when opponents work hard to defend Hodge and other players are freed up for good shots. Hodge can be stopped. In the last 10 regular season games, Hodge was held under 10 points three times—against Virginia, Virginia Tech and Wake Forest. Charlotte may choose to focus on Hodge and make his teammates beat them.

Charlotte has superior scoring balance with three players having double-digit averages—Withers (18 ppg.), Basden (15 ppg.), and Plavich (14 ppg.). Plavich is the three-point shooter who is relied on to pull out the defense. He takes 47% of the team's three-point shots. While less obvious, it might be argued that Charlotte is as dependent on Plavich as North Carolina State is on Hodge. However, Plavich's performance during the last 12 games of the regular season and the Conference USA Tournament is worrisome (See Figure 4-11). His scoring average conceals tremendous highs and lows. He rose to the occasion in some big games against Cincinnati and Louisville, but couldn't hit against TCU, East Carolina and Memphis.

In contrast, Charlotte's big inside threat, Curtis Withers, was a model of consistency in the same 12 games (See Figure 4-12). Withers always scored more than 15 points and hit a high percentage of his shots. However, in 8 of 12 games, Withers committed four fouls but did not foul out. Withers' playing time needs to be managed to keep him in the game. While he may not foul out, foul trouble can limit his upside contribution, particularly in close games. His scoring average in games in which he finished with four fouls is only 21.3, compared to 28.5 in games in which he had fewer than four fouls.

Figure 4-11: Brendan Plavich Scoring Trend

Date	Opponent	Outcome	3 Pt. FGs	Points
1/26/2005	TCU	W	1--8	5
1/29/2005	East Carolina	L	2--7	8
2/5/2005	Cincinnati	W	8--17	26
2/9/2005	Houston	W	6--12	18
2/12/2005	St.Louis	W	3--12	12
2/16/2005	DePaul	W	0--6	7
2/19/2005	Tulane	W	4--10	14
2/23/2005	Memphis	W	4--8	12
2/26/2005	So. Miss	W	2--5	6
3/3/2005	Louisville	L	7--16	28
3/5/2005	S. Florida	L	6--14	20
3/8/2005	Memphis	L	1--10	3

Figure 4-12: Curtis Withers Scoring Trend

Date	Opponent	Outcome	2-Pt Shots	Fouls	Points
1/26/2005	TCU	W	7--11	4	16
1/29/2005	E. Carolina	L	8--20	2	23
2/5/2005	Cincinnati	W	3--8	4	15
2/9/2005	Houston	W	8--13	4	21
2/12/2005	St. Louis	W	13--25	3	39
2/16/2005	DePaul	W	7--12	4	18
2/19/2005	Tulane	W	8--16	1	26
2/23/2005	Memphis	W	6--14	4	20
2/26/2005	So. Miss	W	10--17	3	25
3/3/2005	Louisville	L	7--10	4	20
3/5/2005	S. Florida	L	5--12	4	19
3/8/2005	Memphis	L	11--21	4	32

- ***Depth.*** Lack of team depth is an important consideration in game analysis. A short bench makes a team susceptible to fatigue, injury, foul trouble and overtime. A short bench invites opponents to try to take advantage by applying more pressure. Conversely, a deep bench does not always confer an advantage on a team, except perhaps when it has 9-10 skilled and athletic players and plays an aggressive pressing style.

North Carolina State has adequate depth. Typically, it is very deep, with 10 players getting an average of more than 10 minutes per game. Even if Tony Bethel and Jordon Collins are not at full strength and do not get their normal 40 minutes (combined) playing time, North Carolina State still has sufficient depth for this game. North Carolina State has had plenty of time to rest and prepare for this game.

Charlotte goes eight deep—eight players who average more than 13.4 minutes per game. There are no injuries and the team is rested and has had time to prepare. Charlotte tends to shorten its rotation in tough games. Therefore, it is likely that the starters will all go more than 30 minutes in this game.

Overall, neither team has an advantage with respect to depth and playing rotation.

- *Special Conditions.* You should be alert to special conditions associated with a match-up—conditions that are obvious and potentially material. There are a dozen types of special conditions, ranging from playing on Senior Night to having a team coached by an assistant because the head coach is unavailable.

In this game there are two special conditions worth noting. One condition is Charlotte's desire to prove itself. Charlotte frequently complains that the big teams in North Carolina will not play it, implying that it is too strong for a non-conference opponent. It is not clear that the record justifies this position, but such a posture can certainly improve Charlotte's intensity in this game.

A second condition is the apparent anomaly that North Carolina State is a #10 seed, while Charlotte is a #7 seed. Yet, North Carolina State is favored by four points. To some degree this confuses bettors. Some bettors might view Charlotte as a bargain. Other bettors might see the point spread as evidence that North Carolina State has been getting stronger or Charlotte has been getting weaker. While this anomaly should not affect your analysis and conclusions, it may affect the point spread and provide you with some additional advantage.

Step 6: Draw Conclusions and Make Wagering Decisions

Ultimately, you must look at the results of the various analyses and decide whether Charlotte or North Carolina State is expected to perform better than the prevailing point spread. Will North Carolina State win by more than four points? If so, how much more than four points will it win by?

Unfortunately, you can't just add up a few numbers and reach a reliable answer. You must look at the results of the various analyses and apply knowledge of college basketball to reach actionable conclusions. This is an advantage for knowledgeable fans that put in the effort to study a game, compared to those bettors who simply use mathematical formulas to try to forecast the outcomes of dozens of games each day of the season (see Chapter 3, Section 11).

You should have reasonable expectations and remember that you are wagering for entertainment value as well as to make money. That is, you are a consumer of college basketball entertainment, as well as an investor. The majority of the time you will conclude that the point spread appears fairly accurate and that there is no more than a two- or three-point advantage in taking one of the teams. Your wager will primarily be for entertainment purposes, but over time, those few points will make a significant difference in how often you win.

There will be occasions in which your analysis shows that the point spread is very much off and, therefore, provides you with a large wagering advantage. Those are the situations in which you will behave more like an investor in college basketball. You will place larger wagers and the winnings from those wagers will ensure that you have a highly profitable college basketball season.

Figure 4-13 displays how you can systematically arrange the results of your analyses. This table can be prepared fairly quickly as you conduct the various analyses.

For this game, the ultimate conclusion is that North Carolina State is significantly better than the four point spread. The six key results, drawn from the discussion above and Figure 3-13 that justify a wager on North Carolina State are listed below.

- *North Carolina State is getting stronger more rapidly than is commonly perceived by the wagering public.* While its success in the ACC Tournament is well publicized, North Carolina State's improvement during the last six weeks of the regular season is not well known. It went 7-3 ATS with an average cover margin of 7.85 points. Charlotte is seemingly pegged accurately by bettors, going 4-6 ATS with equal average cover and non-cover margins. Therefore, there is a high probability that the point spread undervalues North Carolina State.

- *North Carolina State performs very well against teams of the caliber of Charlotte;* Charlotte has trouble with teams of the caliber of North Carolina State. North Carolina State not only played many games against teams of Charlotte's caliber, it played at least six games against teams that were far superior. Against teams comparable to Charlotte, North Carolina State went 6-2 straight-up and 6-2 ATS, covering by an average of 11 points. Charlotte has gone 4-2 straight up and 2-4 ATS against teams comparable in strength to North Carolina State, but the point spreads on those games have largely been accurate. North Carolina State's performance on this measure is highly correlated with the metrics for the last 10 regular season games. Nevertheless, this indicator increases confidence that North Carolina State's form against comparable teams will prevail in this match-up.

- *North Carolina State's shooting provides an advantage.* Against comparable opponents, North Carolina State has hit 45% of its three-point field goal attempts and 47% of its two-

Figure 4-13: Summary Analysis of Charlotte vs. North Carolina State

Step 1: Predictability of Game

Mismatch (Point Spread > 12)	No
High Impact Injuries	No
Highly Unusual Playing Conditions (e.g., Venue, Time)	No
Unequal Information Available for Both Teams	No

Step 2: Evaluation of Recent Perfomance Against the Spread (Last 10 Regular Season Games)

	NC State	Charlotte
ATS	7–3	4–6
Cover Margin	7.85 (Consistently Large)	6.25
Non-Cover Margin	8.33 (2 of 3 games vs. UNC)	6.25
Other Considerations	Easily covered 2 of 3 games in ACC Tournament	Early loss in CUSA Tournament

Figure 4-13: Summary Analysis of Charlotte vs. North Carolina State (cont.)

Step 3: Performance Against Comparable Opponents	NC State	Charlotte
Comparable Opponents -- Overall Strength	Virginia Tech Maryland (2) Georgia Tech (2) Clemson Florida State	Louisville Memphis DePaul Cincinnati (2) Alabama-Birmingham
Comparable Opponents -- Style of Play	Georgia Tech	None
Comparable Opponents -- Performance ATS	6--2 (Failures to cover before Jan. 26th)	2--4

Primary Performance Statistics vs. Comparables	NC State - Offense	Charlotte - Defense
Field Goal Pct.	46%	47%
2 Pt Field Goal Pct.	47%	53%
3 Pt. Field Goal Pct	45%	39%
3 Pt. Shots/Total	46%	40%

Figure 4-13: Summary Analysis of Charlotte vs. North Carolina State (cont.)

Step 4: Overall Trends and Home vs. Road Performance

	NC State	Charlotte
Recent Record	5-5 (Losses to UNC(2), Wake Forest (2), Virginia)	9-4 Lost games should have won -- TCU, E Carolina, St. Louis, S. Fla.
ATS Road	5-2	2-5
W-L Road	4-3	3-4

Step 5: Assessing Consistency, Personnel and Other Factors

Consistency -- Key Metrics of Performance

	NC State	Charlotte
Three Point Shooting	High (>38% in 7 of 8 games)	Medium
ATO	High (exceeds ATO of opponent in all 8 games)	Medium
Three Point Defense	Medium (Tendency to letdown vs. lesser teams)	High (All comparable opponents >36%)
Free Throw Attempts	Medium (Tendency to letdown vs. lesser teams)	High (Positive margin in all games)
Scoring Balance	Dependent on Hodge -- 17ppg; five players averaging 7-10 ppg)	Good balance --Withers (18 pg), Pavlich 14 ppg) and Basden (15 ppg)
Vulnerability	Hodge held below 10 points in 3 of last 10 regular seasong games	Pavlich relied on for 3s -- inconsistent; Withers consistent scorer but limited by propensity to foul
Depth	Availability of Bethel and Collins continues to be uncertain, but depth should not be a factor	Typically go 8 deep -- depth should not be a factor
Special Conditions	Charlotte lower seed may send money away from NC State	Charlotte desire to beat in-state competitor

point field goal attempts— excellent offensive performance. Defense is not Charlotte's strength. Comparable opponents hit 53% and 39% of their two and three point shots, respectively. North Carolina State's offense is unlikely to be stopped— it will score with two and three-point shots. Conversely, Charlotte struggles a bit on offense against comparable teams, hitting two- and three-point shots at 42% and 36%, respectively. Charlotte relies on hitting threes to open up the inside. However, North Carolina State has the ability to stop the three and collapse on big men inside. North Carolina State's defense is solid and flexible, so it is unlikely that Charlotte will do better than its averages against comparable opponents.

There is a way to approximate the importance of shooting offense and defense in this game. Both teams are likely to get about 60 shots—there is not a sufficient rebounding or turnover margin to assume a significant difference in field goal attempts. If both teams play to form, in terms of both accuracy and shot selection, their scoring from field goals would be:

North Carolina State

	Accuracy	Pct. Shots	Attempts	Made	Points
2-Pt. Field Goals	47%	54%	32	15	30
3-Pt. Field Goals	45%	46%	28	13	39
Total			60	28	69

Charlotte

	Accuracy	Pct. Shots	Attempts	Made	Points
2-Pt. Field Goals	42%	62%	37	16	32
3-Pt. Field Goals	36%	38%	23	8	24
Total			60	24	56

The estimated difference based on shooting from the field is 13 points. Computing point differences in this way is not exceptionally precise. Therefore, it is more realistic to assume that the point difference is a range of 10-16.

- *Charlotte's free throw margin should diminish the overall scoring differential.* Charlotte has a consistent ability to generate a free throw attempt margin. There is every indication that a 6-9 free throw attempt margin will be generated in this game—translating to 4-6 points in the final score. Adjusting the scoring difference from field goals to reflect free throws, the likely net scoring differential is 4-12 points. The low end of the range corresponds to the point spread prevailing in the market. This indicates a very good wagering opportunity.

- *North Carolina State is a superior ball-handling team as measured by ATO.* Its advantage (1.33 vs. .76) against comparable opponents is superior to Charlotte (.99 vs. 1.11). Looking at the components—assists and turnovers—there are two conclusions. First, North Carolina State's small turnover margin is not material. Second, its assists margin simply reinforces conclusions regarding the certainty of North Carolina State achieving a substantial scoring differential.

- *Scoring balance will be a test of defensive strategies and will.* Both teams will undertake a strategy to reduce the opponent's scoring. These strategies can be predicted with reasonable accuracy. The relative effectiveness of each strategy will cause variances from each team's historical performance metrics and affect the scoring differential between the two teams. While largely a matter of judgment, Charlotte is a bit more vulnerable than North Carolina State. This is a conclusion based on the analysis that will be different than the perception of the majority of bettors who simply assume that stopping Hodge is the way to stop North Carolina State. But, considering Charlotte's scoring patterns, it is critically dependent on both Plavich hitting from the outside and Withers playing at least 35 minutes unencumbered by four fouls. The chances of North Carolina

State stopping Plavich or Withers are greater than Charlotte stopping Hodge.

In, summary when everything is considered, it seems clear that North Carolina State will cover the four points and that the expected differential is in the 8-10 point range. This advantage makes the wager on this game a legitimate investment—one that justifies more than the average wager—rather than primarily a source of entertainment.

The Results of the Game

North Carolina State won the game 75-63—covering the four-point spread by eight.

On the surface, it would appear that it played out perfectly. A cover margin of eight is a convincing victory. However, a quick look at the game's box score (Figure 4-14) might give a contrary impression -- that luck played a big role in the victory rather than effective handicapping.

It would have been easy to have devoted this chapter to a game that played out precisely as forecast. There certainly are such games. However, the purpose of this example is to demonstrate three important things about handicapping. First, the North Carolina State vs. Charlotte game shows that while there are uncertainties in important college basketball games and there is an ebb and flow, 40 minutes is sufficient time for the class and form of teams to prevail. Second, the game shows the value of thorough analysis. Even if North Carolina State did not cover, there was a clear indication that it was the team on which to place a wager. As noted earlier, while you might expect to win 60% of your wagers, you should ensure that you do a good job handicapping 80% of the games. Finally, it shows the value of analyzing the outcome of the game, even when it seems that you have won handily.

Figure 4-14: Box Score -- North Carolina State vs. Charlotte

North Carolina State								
Players	MIN	FGM-A	FTM-A	OFF	REB	AST	PF	PTS
J. Hodge, G-F	40	8--12	3--4	3	7	9	0	19
A. Brackman, F	24	4--10	8--8	5	6	2	1	16
I. Evtimov, F	37	2--7	6--6	0	4	0	4	12
C. Bennerman, G-F	35	5--12	1--2	0	4	0	2	12
E. Atsur, G	38	4--7	1--2	1	4	2	0	10
G. Grant, G-F	7	2--6	0-0	1	2	1	0	4
L. Watkins, F	6	0-1	0-0	0	0	0	1	0
C. Simmons, F-C	13	1--4	0-0	1	3	0	2	2
		26-59	19-22	11	30	14	10	75
		44.10%	86.40%					

TEAM REBS: 30

TURNOVERS: 16 (I Evtimov 4, L Watkins 1, J Hodge 2, C Bennerman 2, E Atsur 3, A Brackman 1, G Grant 1, C Simmons 2)
BLOCKED SHOTS: 8 (J Hodge 1, C Bennerman 1, E Atsur 1, A Brackman 4, C Simmons 1)

STEALS: 14 (I Evtimov 4, J Hodge 3, C Bennerman 3, E Atsur 2, C Simmons 2)

3-PT FGS: 4-19, .211 (I Evtimov 2-6, L Watkins 0-1, J Hodge 0-2, C Bennerman 1-5, E Atsur 1-3, A Brackman 0-1, G Grant 0-1)

CHARLOTTE 49ERS								
Players	MIN	FGM-A	FTM-A	OFF	REB	AST	PF	PTS
E. Drayton, F	31	5--9	0-0	2	9	1	2	11
C. Withers, F	37	6--14	3--6	1	5	2	5	15
E. Basden, F	40	5--14	4--6	3	10	4	2	15
B. Plavich, G	36	5--10	0-0	0	2	1	2	15
M. Baldwin, G	32	1--1	2--2	0	2	2	0	4
C. Nance, F	3	0-1	0-0	0	0	0	2	0
M. Iti, C	9	0-2	0-0	1	2	1	3	0
L. Goldwire, G	12	1--7	0-0	1	2	0	2	3
		23-58	9--14	8	32	11	18	63
		39.70%	64.30%					

TEAM REBS: 32
TURNOVERS: 19 (B Plavich 3, E Basden 4, M Baldwin 3, C Withers 7, M Iti 1, E Drayton 1)
BLOCKED SHOTS: 2 (C Withers 1, E Drayton 1)
STEALS: 8 (B Plavich 2, E Basden 2, M Baldwin 1, C Withers 1, L Goldwire 2)
3-PT FGS: 8-21, .381 (B Plavich 5-10, E Basden 1-3, C Withers 0-2, L Goldwire 1-3, E Drayton 1-3)

This game was a tale of two halves. Charlotte started very hot, executing its strategy perfectly. Specifically, the strategy was to have Plavich hit threes and open up the inside for Withers and Basden. At the same time, it was to stop North Carolina State's perimeter shooting to ensure that it did not fall behind early. Until a timeout at 6:55 of the first half, North Carolina State was completely outplayed and trailed by 12 points (27-15). The scoring statistics for the first 13:05 were:

	NC State	Charlotte
2-Pt. Field Goals—Attempts	10	11
2-Pt. Field Goals—Made	4	6
2-Pt. Field Goals—Pct.	40%	54%
3-Pt. Field Goals—Attempts	7	7
3-Pt. Field Goals—Made	1	5
3-Pt. Field Goals—Pct.	14%	71%
Free Throw Points	4	0
Points	15	27

Charlotte hit 11 of its first 18 shots. Plavich has made all four of his three-point attempts, and four baskets were the result of lay-ups and dunks. At the same time, North Carolina State hit only 5 of 17 from the floor including only one three-point field goal. Turnovers and rebounds were not factors. The first third of the game was about shooting, and the early results were precisely the opposite of those that were expected.

For the remainder of the first half and the entire second half, the game was entirely different. North Carolina State won the final 27 minutes by 24 points, 60-36. The scoring statistics for that period are shown below.

	NC State	Charlotte
2-Pt. Field Goals—Attempts	30	26
2-Pt. Field Goals—Made	18	9
2-Pt. Field Goals—Pct.	60%	35%
3-Pt. Field Goals—Attempts	12	14
3-Pt. Field Goals—Made	3	3
3-Pt. Field Goals—Pct.	25%	21%
Free Throw Points	15	8
Points	60	36

North Carolina State and Charlotte both reverted to form—the form that had been anticipated for this game. North Carolina State focused on Plavich and he hit one of six shots in the remaining 27 minutes. The interior defense became more intense and Charlotte hit only 35% of its two point shots. Overall, in the final 27 minutes of the game, Charlotte hit only 30% from the floor. Withers was held to 15 points—the lowest of any of the comparable games—and ultimately fouled out.

At the same time, North Carolina State's offense improved dramatically. It had done a good job of distributing the ball during the first 13 minutes—Hodge only took two shots. The other starters got good shots but simply could not hit them. However, in the final 27 minutes the players seemed to get comfortable and hit 50% of their shots. Ultimately, Hodge with 19 points on 12 attempts was only one of five double-figure scorers for North Carolina State—excellent scoring balance.

Rather than rely on the three, North Carolina State confidently worked for higher percentage shots inside, hitting 60% of two-point field goal attempts and drawing fouls. Only 28% of North Carolina State's shots during this period were from behind the arc. This was the right strategy considering the experience Charlotte had had against comparable teams. Those teams hit 53% of their two-point field goal attempts and did not need to rely much on the three.

Finally, contrary to expectations, North Carolina State gained an advantage in free throw attempts, 15-8. This was a result of two things. First, North Carolina State was careful not to foul. Second, the free throw attempt margin was generated in the last two minutes of the game as Charlotte fouled to gain possession. North Carolina State had nine free throw attempts in that short period.

In summary, ultimately the factors that were forecast as the most important discriminators between the two teams – shooting offense and defense and, also, scoring balance – made the difference. North Carolina State was a much stronger team and overcame Charlotte's game strategy.

5. Summary

Fans who wager on college basketball can be consistent winners while still gaining the full entertainment value of both the games and wagering.

To do so it is only necessary to do four things:

- Focus almost exclusively on point-spread wagering

- Invest about 15-20 minutes to analyze each game using an intelligent standardized handicapping approach

- Vary the amounts wagered to reflect your perceived advantage—the difference between the outcome you forecast for the game and the point spread

- Shop among sports books for the most favorable terms—both the point spread and the moneyline on the wager.

How successful can you be? It is possible to win 60% of your point-spread bets. You will win 50% of the time if you simply flip a coin to decide the teams on which to wager. If you use an intelligent handicapping approach, you can win an additional one time in 10. Doing so has a major impact on the amount of your winnings. Suppose you start with a bankroll of $1,000 and make fifty $110 wagers. If you win 60% of the wagers, at the end of the season you will have your original $1,000 bankroll, $800 in winnings—an 80% return on your bankroll in about four months—plus $5,500 in wagering entertainment.

The thing that makes your bankroll more powerful in wagering on college basketball is that you can use the same money over and over again during the season. It is possible to put money at risk and win within 24 hours. Winnings compound rapidly when you win 60% of your bets while using the same money over and over again. This is in stark contrast to investments such as stocks and bonds in which you tie up your money in an asset until you sell it and a 10% annual return is considered good.

Most people think that they are wagering against the sports book—trying to beat all-knowing line makers. In point-spread wagering, the sports book really acts more like an exchange, or intermediary, matching your wager with someone who is willing to take the other side of the wager. While a line maker establishes the opening point spread, the final point spread really represents the consensus of the wagering public—the dollars wagered on the game are split fairly evenly between the two sides of the point spread.

The primary reason that you should be able to win 60% of your wagers is that you are largely wagering against people like yourself, many of whom are wagering solely for entertainment. If you put in a bit more effort and handicap a game a bit more intelligently than most of those people, you will gain a substantial advantage and win more often. While there are professional sports bettors, they do not dominate college basketball wagering and you should not be intimated by them. Even if you cannot beat the professionals, there is plenty of money to be made by beating amateurs!

One of the reasons that professionals do not dominate college basketball wagering is that there are commonly 300-400 games to wager on during each week of the season, so professionals spread their wagers across many games. This is in sharp contrast to the NFL, college football or professional basketball in which the wagering of professionals is highly concentrated in relatively few games. As a result, the mix of your wagering competition varies enormously between games—sometimes heavily influenced by professionals, and at other times, limited to amateurs.

The focus of this book is point-spread wagering. The reasons for specializing in this type of proposition are that it is the most common proposition—every sports book offers it; it most coincides with the way most people watch a game and root for teams; it has the lowest vigorish (commissions for the sports book)—which is being driven lower by competition among sports book and, also, an advantage can be reliably gained by applying an intelligent handicapping methodology.

Wagering on college basketball has exploded in recent years because of the availability and accessibility of offshore sports books in addition to those in Nevada. These sports books act like other types of exchanges. The terms of propositions are posted and those of one sports book can be compared to others. You can maintain accounts with sports books as you would with your stock broker. The openness of sports wagering is putting the traditional local bookie out of business since the only advantage a bookie can offer now is credit—something that the vast majority of those who wager on sports do not need or desire.

Overall, the integrity of college basketball wagering is as high as other traditional forms of investment such as stocks, bonds, real estate and art. There are many constituencies that have an interest in a clean sport and a wagering market with high integrity. The NCAA, college and university administrators, coaches and players, all recognizing the potential impact on the sport, are vigilant in preventing point shaving or game fixing. Similarly, sports books have a similar incentive—not so much because of a potential loss from a fixed game, but because diminished integrity of any sport will substantially reduce the overall level of wagering on it.

Similarly, there have been questions about the integrity of offshore sports books. Today sports books are a significant part of the economies in several countries in the Caribbean and Central America. Governments in those countries license their sports books and go to some effort to ensure liquidity. Also, with so many sports books to choose from, those that are not reputable are quickly weeded out. You will not encounter much financial risk in maintaining accounts with reputable offshore sports books.

There is an increasing amount of competition among sports books that works to the benefit of the bettor. Sports books compete on the basis of the propositions they handle, their moneyline terms (commissions and fees), when they begin taking money on a game and bettor loyalty programs. When you select sports books with which to set up accounts it is useful to compare their features and select those that best meet your wagering needs.

There is one other thing that has recently had a huge impact on college basketball wagering: the availability of information. The Internet has leveled the playing field with respect to information. Websites provided by colleges and universities, as well as sports media and statistical services, provide comprehensive data on each team and its players. You can easily have access to as much information as professionals and virtually all of the information that will have a bearing on forecasting the outcomes of games. This is in contrast to the situation that used to exist, in which information was not easily obtained. A little "inside information" could make a big difference in how one would wager, but that information was generally only available to people who made a business of wagering on college basketball.

There are four critical skills in wagering on college basketball. To win consistently, you must be competent in all four.

Analysis: Forecasting Game Outcomes. Your advantage in point-spread wagering is derived from anticipating when the outcome of a game is likely to be different than the point spread. The larger the difference between the two, the bigger the potential wagering advantage. Therefore, the ability to understand what causes game outcomes and to intelligently use past performance to forecast the future is critical.

Information: Finding and Managing Valuable Data. Information regarding college basketball teams and players is readily available. The challenge today is to not be overwhelmed by too much information. You must decide what data is needed to support the way you do analysis, identify its sources, and then put in place the means of efficiently obtaining, storing, manipulating and displaying it. This can be done fairly easily with a personal computer, browser, spreadsheet program and Internet connection. You don't want to have to spend much time searching for data and manipulating it—you should be spending your time analyzing games.

Money Management. It's important to deploy your bankroll in a way that balances your desire to consistently win a lot of money with the risk of losing all of your money. You must be sure that the entertainment of wagering on college basketball does not overwhelm sound financial management and judgment. The most important principle of money management is to vary the amount of your wagers to reflect the advantage that you think you have based on your analysis, recognizing that less than half of the games will provide good wagering opportunities and only about 10% will be outstanding opportunities to win big.

Discipline. The greatest threat to your success is lack of discipline. When you are making wagers for both entertainment and to win money, it is sometimes hard to balance the two. You might desire more entertainment and wager accordingly. That is fine as long you know you are doing it deliberately and do not also expect big winnings. The greater risk is when poor logic undermines wagering discipline. For example, wagering more during a losing streak because you are "due to win" represents a lack of discipline based on a false premise.

The biggest difference between people who consistently win and those who lose is their ability to analyze college basketball games. As noted earlier, in point-spread wagering you gain an advantage when you find games in which the outcome you forecast differs from the point spread. The average variance between game outcomes and point spreads ranges from seven to 10 points, depending on

139

the conference. Therefore, there is plenty of opportunity to find differences and turn them into profitable wagers.

There are six steps in analyzing games and making wagering decisions. The first step is testing whether it is possible to forecast the outcome of a game. There are certain situations in which the outcomes of games relative to the expectations of the wagering public cannot be reliably determined. So there is little point in wasting time doing analysis or placing a significant amount of money at risk. These conditions tend to be: (1) mismatches, in which one team is favored by more than 10-12 points; (2) lineups and rotations altered due to injury or suspension; (3) strange locations or playing venues; and (4) very early season games.

Once you eliminate unpredictable games from consideration (Step 1), there are five steps in game analysis.

Step 2   Evaluate recent performance against the spread

Step 3:   Assess performance against comparable opponents

Step 4:   Assess trends and home vs. away advantage

Step 5:   Assess consistency, personnel and other factors

Step 6:   Draw conclusions and make wagering decisions

The most important elements of these steps are described below.

Analysis of Trends

All but the most casual bettors use a team's past performance to forecast the future. There is merit in the overall concept. On average, a team's performance in the next game will be a lot like those in prior games. Being able to accurately forecast the future provides an advantage.

There are several aspects of doing this that are particularly important. First, only games played in the prior five or six weeks—

approximately 10-12 games—are relevant. They are the best indicators of current performance. Games played in November are irrelevant in February. Second, looking at 10-12 games is the means of identifying broad trends—team improvement or deteriorating performance. Third, this set of games allows you to determine what accounts for a team's performance and whether those conditions will be perpetuated in future games. For example, if the next game is on the road against a superior team, the predictive value of prior games may be diminished if those games were largely at home against lesser teams.

The real power in forecasting is identifying situations in which a team's performance in the next game is likely to be different than most bettors expect. When the play of two teams has been highly consistent, that will be apparent to many bettors. Many bettors will choose sides and place wagers based on the expectation that that consistency will be perpetuated in the next game—and most of the time they will be right in doing so. It is hard to gain a large advantage. However, when you can identify situations in which performance is changing rapidly and isolate factors that will make the next game different than past games, you can gain a large wagering advantage. The good news is that identifying these situations entails the type of basketball knowledge that you probably have, rather than complex manipulations of data and the application of sophisticated statistical techniques.

The last three or four games played frequently provide reliable indicators of change. Changes in starting lineup and rotation, shot selection, defensive strategy and execution, and point guard play can be identified and potentially extrapolated to future games. But, it is important that those were the factors that truly influenced the team's recent performance. Sometimes, playing lesser opponents or home court advantage gives the impression of change.

The best and most easily identified indicator of a team's trend is performance against the point spread. The performance against the point spread indicates how the team has done relative to the expectations of the wagering public—your competition. Bettors commonly only look at how often a team covered or failed to cover the spread. However, a more powerful indicator that is not commonly considered is "cover margin"—when a team covers, how much does it cover by? When it fails to cover, by how much does it fail to cover? This can be a big discriminator between two teams that have both gone 5-5 against the spread. Also, it is a means of determining how strong a team that has done very well against the spread really is, or whether a few narrow covers distort its apparent performance.

Performance Against Comparable Opponents

The best indicator of how a team will play against a specific opponent is the way that it has played against recent opponents of similar strength and playing style. In handicapping college basketball games, averages can be very deceiving. In most cases, the next opponent is not going to play like the average of all prior opponents. So, cumulative season statistics are not exceptionally reliable indicators of performance. You need to identify the prior games against opponents whose strength was similar to the current opponent—as indicated by any reputable power rating—and/or have a similar playing style.

Once you identify past games against comparable opponents, you can look at the statistics that are the best indicators of game outcomes. There are a handful of measures that characterize how a team has played—on both offense and defense. These measures pertain to:

- Field goal scoring—two-point and three-point field goals
- Ball handling—primarily turnovers and assists
- Rebounding
- Free throw attempts

There are three important things to look at. You must look at how each team's offense matches up with the opponent's defense and vice versa. For example, finding a team that shoots threes particularly well playing against a team that has a poor perimeter defense provides an advantage. Similarly, finding a team that has an aggressive defense and forces lots of turnovers playing against a team with poor ball handling skills provides an advantage.

Second, you must look for consistency of performance and ensure that averages for these games are not deceiving. For example, overall, a team may hit a high percentage of its three-point shots against comparable opponents, but run hot and cold so that the average is meaningless. In looking at comparables, consistency is your friend!

Finally, a high percentage of people wagering look primarily at cumulative season averages and place their bets accordingly. It's worth looking at the difference between cumulative season averages and the averages for comparable games. The greater the difference, the greater the potential advantage you will have relative to the point spread. Your assessment of how teams match up will almost always be more reliable than that of people who use cumulative season averages.

Other Material Factors

There are several other attributes of teams and their play which are material. These factors validate your selection of the team on which to wager and tend to have a larger impact on assessing how much of an advantage you have relative to the point spread, and therefore, how much to wager.

- Home vs. away—indications of particular strength or weakness at home or on the road which help calibrate the home court advantage. Home court advantage typically ranges from two to five points.
- Scoring balance—the degree to which scoring is distributed among starters for the two teams relative to the stringency of their defenses.

- Depth—the relative depth of the teams and identification of those situations in which differences may have an impact on strategy and performance.

- Special condition—game-specific conditions that may affect outcomes but were not present in prior games during the season.

When the analysis has been completed the real question is: How much difference is there between the likely outcome of the game and the point spread? There is no simple mechanical way to get the answer. It is not a question of adding up a few numbers.

The key is to highlight the differences in the two teams and determine how that translates into the play of the game and outcomes. You are primarily looking for strengths matched against weaknesses, consistency matched against inconsistency, positive trends matched against negative trends. It is not possible to convert each of these differences to a difference in points. Rather, you must look at all the differences and judge the range of points that they might translate to.

Keep in mind what you are really trying to do. You are not looking for situations in which a four-point spread should really be a five point spread—no handicapping methodology has that level of precision, whether you spend 20 minutes or 20 hours analyzing a game. You are trying to make grosser distinctions that determine the amount of money to place at risk. Is the four-point spread accurate such that the game doesn't really provide a good wagering opportunity? Should the four-point spread really be a spread of five to eight points such that it provides a good wagering opportunity? Should the four-point spread be more than eight points such that it provides a very good opportunity? The ability to make distinctions at this level is well within your capability based on the analyses performed and will guide wagering so as to achieve a high win rate.

There is one note of caution when doing your analysis and drawing conclusions from results. There is frequently a positive correlation among the factors that you analyze—that is, if one is rated highly, then some of the others also tend to be rated highly because they are caused by the same thing. This tends to create a bias for the favorite. The favorite will appear to have a greater advantage relative to the underdog than is really the case. Therefore, you should be alert as to what amounts to some double counting and be sure to fairly evaluate underdogs before wagering on favorites. In general, there is more money made from underdogs than favorites because casual handicappers find it harder to see how an underdog will cover. Don't fall into the same trap as your competitors.

Finally, you should understand the outcome of every wager, win or lose. There is a temptation to ignore losers and bask in the glory of winners. But, you should learn from both and improve both your skills and efficiency over time. You must remember that you can't control the outcome of games, but you can control the quality of your handicapping and your wagers. An acceptable outcome is doing a good job in handicapping the game and making the right wager, but losing because the teams did not play to form. That is quite different than losing because you did a poor job in handicapping the game and never had much of a chance to win. While you will be doing well if you win 60% of your wagers, you must satisfy yourself that 80% of the time you have properly handicapped the game and made an appropriate wager.

Finally, intelligently wagering on college basketball will provide both fun and profit. Over time, you will handicap more quickly and have greater insight, bet more precisely and win more frequently. You can become a consistent winner.

About the Author

Larry Seidel is an expert on wagering on college basketball. His successful wagering techniques utilize many of the basic principles of finance and market economics. His last book, **Investing in College Basketball**, described a comprehensive methodology by which serious bettors on college basketball could realize returns on their "investments" that were far greater than conventional investments such as stocks and bonds. Mr. Seidel has run large management and information technology consulting businesses serving the banking and financial services industry. He earned degrees in economics and finance from the University of Chicago.